THE
CHARTERSVILLE
STORY

AUTHORED BY:
WILLIAM LEWTON

ISBN-13: 978-0-615-54561-5

In Memory Of

William R. Lewton
October 11, 1927 – October 11, 2011

Loving father and provider to seven children.

THE
CHARTERSVILLE
STORY

Chapter 1

"Bye, Justin," Dad said as he pulled the apartment door closed and locked it from the outside.

Steven and Fran were always slightly apprehensive about leaving Justin on his own, Steven more so than Fran. Justin had a form of Autism and was prone to doing things most people would not, simple things like putting ice cream in the refrigerator instead of the freezer, or forgetting to turn the burner off after making soup; however, Justin had just turned sixteen and, in the past couple of years had seemed to become more responsible. Steven and Fran felt more comfortable about leaving him on his own for short periods of time now.

Steven and Fran walked up the steps to the apartment complex parking lot and Steven, who always drove when Fran was with him, got in, fastened his seat belt, and started the car. It was hot outside already, and Steven wanted the air conditioning on full blast, even for the short drive to the Waffle Haven where he and Fran intended to have breakfast. He turned right out of the apartment complex, and right again, onto Monterey Boulevard, a usually very busy, three-lane, divided city street. At the next light, he turned right again, onto Trolens, another divided highway not usually as busy as Monterey Boulevard. It had its share of traffic, too, though.

What was unusual about this trip was that Steven and Fran seemed to be the only car on the road. Steven commented on this; however, he dismissed it to being a Sunday morning. Light after light, Steven and Fran's car was the only one on the road.

That's when Steven made the comment, "Okay, this is weird."

Fran agreed.

When Steven made it to Centers Avenue, he turned right on Centers, and Waffle Haven was just a few hundred feet down the road on the right, still not a car on the road.

Just after turning right onto Centers, Steven heard a very loud, short siren, looked in his rear view mirror to see a city police car with flashers on directly behind him, and heard the officer's voice over the loudspeaker saying, "Driver, stop the car immediately. Do not roll down the windows, and do not exit the vehicle. Driver, keep your hands on the steering wheel. Passenger, keep your hands on the dash."

At that moment, a second city patrol car pulled directly in front of Steven's vehicle in an effort to keep Steven from leaving. Fran, now in what seemed to be a kind of stunned, but very rational state, immediately noticed that neither officer was exiting their vehicle to talk to either of them. Fran had always had an uncanny ability to think very rationally in a step-by-step, common sense approach in what she perceived to be an emergency situation, a quality she did not possess under normal circumstances. Steven, on the other hand, had always reacted frantically when faced with an emergency and possessed common sense and rationality only when life was taking its normal course.

In what seemed like just seconds later, a fire engine pulled along side Steven's now boxed-in car. Each occupant of the fire engine, two on the inside, and four on the outside, was dressed in what appeared to be bio-chemical protection suits.

Two members of this group approached Steven and Fran's car, one on each side, knocked on the windows, and asked the same questions of both Steven and Fran, "How do you feel? Are you experiencing any nausea or lightheadedness?"

Both Steven and Fran responded that they did not.

Only after asking Steven, "Are you sure you both feel fine? No unusual feelings whatsoever?" did the same gentlemen state, "Listen, the officer behind you is going to give you some instructions over the loudspeaker. I want you to follow his instructions very carefully. Do not open your windows, and do not exit the vehicle until you are instructed to do so."

As the firemen returned to the engine, the officer behind Steven's car once again speaking over the loudspeaker stated, "Driver, listen to my instructions carefully. Do not roll down your windows, and do not exit the vehicle. I want you to follow the officer in front of you. Do not deviate from his route, and do not exit the vehicle until you are instructed to do so."

With Steven's car still boxed in by the fire engine on the side and the patrol car behind, the patrol car in front of Steven's car backed up and positioned itself directly in front of Steven's car. With flashers still on on both patrol cars, Steven followed the patrol car as instructed.

The drive down Centers Avenue was familiar, as both Steven and Fran had driven it many times before. This time, however, Steven's car and the patrol cars directly behind and in front of the vehicle, as well as the fire engine, were the only cars on the road. Light after light, not a car on the road, and Fran's silence was making Steven feel uncomfortable.

He attempted to reassure her by saying, "Everything's going to be alright, Fran. God has always protected us in the past, and He will now."

Fran remained silent, which in the past had been a sign that she disagreed with Steven, however, did not want to be defensive about it.

After what seemed like a long drive down Centers Avenue, Steven and Fran entered the city's downtown area, following the patrol car, making a right on Second Street and a left on Martin Avenue, a one-way street. Crossing Third Street, the patrol car veered left into a parking garage. Steven recognized this garage, as he had been here several times before. The city's government offices were directly above. As Steven followed the patrol car, which had now turned off its flashers, as well as the one behind them, Steven and Fran's car descended to the lower level, and then again to a lower level, this time with a gate that said "AUTHORIZED VEHICLES ONLY".

Fran finally broke her silence with "I wonder where they're taking us."

Steven responded with a simple, "I don't know."

All three vehicles descended yet another level and came to a stop in front of a metal, roll-up garage door. The officer in front of Steven picked up his radio microphone, and after about a minute, the door opened. After driving through, the door closed behind the patrol car in the rear. The vehicles continued to descend, level after level. This time there were no parking decks, only a concrete drive down that zig-zagged downward with just enough space to turn a vehicle to descend down to the next level and repeat. After six levels down, all three vehicles came to a stop in front of another garage door. The officer in front did not pick up his microphone this time, but after a few minutes, the garage opened.

Steven and Fran now felt very uncomfortable about continuing this journey; however, under the circumstances, they had no choice. This time, the drive was level as all three cars entered and the door closed behind them again. This time, the area inside was very well-lit, and after a short distance, Steven approached another door, a large metal door that slid open from each side. After entering, Steven could see what appeared to be one-way mirrors along the entire length of the room, and another sliding door in front of the front patrol car. Steven and Fran heard yet another voice over the loudspeaker, this time not from the officer behind them.

The voice stated once again, "Driver, Passenger, do not roll down your windows, and do not exit the vehicle."

Once again, about six people dressed in what seemed to be bio-chemical suits entered the area from what seemed to be metal doors, without handles, on each end of the room. This time, the men and women in the suits were carrying what appeared to be sanitizing wands that can be seen in a hospital or sold in drugstores.

Once again, two of the people in the suits approached Steven and Fran's car, one on each side, and asked both Steven and Fran the same questions, "How do you feel? Are you experiencing any nausea or lightheadedness?" to which both Steven and Fran once again responded that they did not.

As these two were asking questions, the other four were passing their wands over the sides, roof, hood, and trunk of the car. Only after the men and women exited the area from the same doors they came in, which seemed to open automatically from the other side for them, and then shut, did the second sliding metal door open. Upon driving through this next door, and the door shutting behind the patrol car in the rear, did all three vehicles come to a stop, again in a very well-lit room with a white tile floor.

At that point, the officer in the patrol car behind them stated over the loudspeaker, "Driver, Passenger, stay in your vehicle until you are instructed to exit," which finally offered a shimmer of hope that this whole experience might be coming to an end; however, as Steven and Fran were about to find out, it was only going to get more complicated.

Chapter 2

Finally, the officer behind them exited his vehicle as another man in a blue suit approached Steven and Fran's car from the driver's side, along with the officer that was behind them.

Once approaching the vehicle, the man wearing the blue suit asked Steven through the window, "What's your name?" Steven replied, and the man then said, "Steven, I want you to open your door from the inside just a crack, no more than an inch or two."

Reaching into his right suit-coat pocket and pulling out what appeared to be a cell phone, the man flipped the device open and held it next to the cracked-open driver's door. The man flipped the device closed and put it back in his pocket.

He then opened the door fully and said, "Steven, you can exit the vehicle now."

At that moment, the officer who was in the patrol car in front of Steven and Fran opened the passenger's side door and stated to Fran, "Passenger, you may exit the vehicle now."

The man in the blue suit identified himself to Steven as John Clemens, the city's bio-hazard safety director, a name and title neither Steven nor Fran had ever heard before. He further stated that he would explain everything in "due time" and asked the two to follow him. Both Steven and Fran were thinking to themselves that as far as they were concerned, "due time" was right now.

After leading Steven and Fran through a door and down a hallway, they came to a series of doors on the right side of the hallway. One of the two officers who had accompanied Mr.

Clemens, Steven, and Fran opened one of these doors. Then Mr. Clemens motioned for Steven and Fran to enter the room. It took only a second for both Steven and Fran to realize that the door locked behind them. Fran and Steven both knew it had, but Steven's natural instincts lead him to try the door in the hope that it would open anyway.

Fran thought to herself, "Where were those instincts when this ordeal first began?"

The room was set up much in the same fashion as a doctor's exam room. It had an examining table, a counter with a sink, and cabinets above the counter. There were two metal stools in the corner of the room. There were no reading materials or medical charts on the wall, as one might expect to find in a doctor's exam room, though. There was also no clock on the wall, and that is when Steven realized he had left his cell phone in the car.

As time passed, it seemed like an eternity. Eventually, the door opened, and Mr. Clemens entered the room, accompanied by a woman who appeared to be in her mid-thirties. She was wearing a white dress, which could pass for a nurse's uniform, but obviously was not. As the door opened, and before it closed again, Steven could not help catching a glimpse of a man standing directly outside the door, wearing what appeared to be a security guard's uniform.

Mr. Clemens began to speak, "Steven, Fran, can you tell me why you two did not heed our warnings to stay indoors and not to leave your homes until you were told it was safe to do so?"

Steven answered with a question, "What warnings?"

Mr. Clemens looked at the woman that was with him, and she began to speak, looking directly at him, saying, "We alerted every TV and radio station in the city and also activated the emergency broadcast system."

Mr. Clemens once again looked at Steven and Fran and asked, "How is it that you did not hear any of these warnings?"

Fran answered him, saying, "We got up and left for breakfast. Justin was reading, and we didn't turn the radio on when we got in the car." There was a short pause from Fran, and then she said, "Oh my God, Justin!"

Mr. Clemens said, "Who is Justin?"

"He's my sixteen-year-old son."

"Don't worry, he's sixteen. He can take care of himself. If he doesn't have the TV or radio on, we have officers and fire department personnel warning the public."

"You don't understand. My son has Autism. He's not going to heed your warnings. We've got to get out of here."

"No one is going anywhere. Early this morning, the city's bio-hazard safety office received a phone call stating that an airborne virus had been released just southwest of the city. We cannot tell you what the virus is, but we can tell you it is potentially life-threatening."

"What about my son?"

"If he heeds our warnings, he'll be fine."

"I just told you he's not going to do that."

At that point, Mr. Clemens and the woman that was with him left the room.

As the door closed, Fran looked at Steven and said, "We have to get out of here."

Chapter 3

Steven looked at Fran and said, "How? There's no window, and there's a guard outside the door, even if we could open it."

Fran looked up at the suspended ceiling.

Steven looked at her and said, "It's a suspended ceiling. You can't walk on that."

Fran looked down at the floor.

Steven knew this look well, and feeling obligated to help, told Fran, "Let me get up on the counter, and I'll lift up a ceiling tile and see what's up their."

To Steven's astonishment, there was a drain pipe just above the ceiling tiles at the end of the counter. It appeared to run parallel to the hallway.

Steven told Fran in his usual managerial way, "This is what we're going to do. See that pipe up there? I want you to stand on the edge of the counter. The pipe is going to be just out of your reach. You've got one shot at this. Jump up and grab the pipe and shimmy toward your right. Keep going until I tell you to stop, and *don't fall*!"

To Steven's amazement, Fran was able to grab the pipe on the first jump. After she had her arm securely around the pipe, she pulled her legs up around the pipe, giving a new meaning to the term leg-locked. She slowly began to shimmy her way down the pipe. When she was just out of the way, Steven attempted the same jump, but his left arm didn't quite make it around the pipe. His right arm caught the pipe on the inside of the elbow. He was able to successfully grasp his left hand with his right, but his right arm hurt where it wrapped around the pipe. Not able to wrap his legs around the pipe like Fran did, Steven shimmied along the pipe just behind Fran, holding his legs just above the ceiling. After shimmying only about thirty feet, Fran knew she was losing her grip, and for this reason, let go of the leg-lock she had around the pipe. Immediately after doing so, she fell through the ceiling. Steven, not wanting to yell, continued to shimmy to the hole, and jumped to the floor below. He immediately asked Fran if she was okay.

Fran replied, "Yeah, I'm fine."

Steven and Fran found themselves in a room just like the previous one. This time the door was unlocked and there was no security guard outside. Steven opened the door slowly. He looked to his left and saw the same security guard standing outside the door of the room they were just in. This time the security guard was talking to another. Steven looked to the right and saw no one. He assumed that this might be the changing of the guard.

He slowly closed the door, and told Fran, "We have to wait here for a few minutes."

Fran, in her usual impatient way, said "Let's go."

"Not yet."

After a few minutes, Steven opened the door again, looked to his left and saw only one guard again, this time reading a magazine. Looking to the right, he again saw nothing except an empty hallway. At the end of the hallway, there was a door. It couldn't have been more than fifteen feet. He looked at Fran, put his index finger over his lip, signaling her to be very quiet, and motioned for her to come toward him.

Steven whispered to Fran, "Go to the right."

As Fran left, Steven shut the door behind him very quietly. The guard was still wrapped up in his magazine and, astonishingly, Steven and Fran were able to make it to the door at the end of the hall without being noticed. Luck was on their side, as the door was not locked, and Steven was able to open it. He opened it just enough for Fran to slip through it first, and himself next, with Steven again shutting the door quietly.

Again, there was a hallway. This one had no doors on either side, and a door at the end of the hallway.

Fran tried this door and said, "It's locked."

Steven said, "Let me try."

After pulling down on the handle, Steven noticed there was a latch at the base of the handle. He held the latch open while pulling down on the handle at the same time, and the door opened, to yet another hallway, this one poorly lit.

Steven and Fran followed the hallway, which seemed to end at what appeared to be a set of sliding chrome doors. These looked to be the doors to an elevator, and Steven and Fran had every intention of using it. The only problem was that there did not seem to be any buttons to push to use the elevator, only a pull-down latch on the wall next to it that read, "PULL FOR EMERGENCY".

Out of options, and taking the biggest chance Steven had taken yet, he pulled the lever down and hoped for the best. The doors opened, and they entered the elevator and pushed the button that said "GL", hoping that it meant ground level. It did, but just before the doors opened, Steven couldn't help but notice the camera in the corner of the elevator above them. As the elevator door opened, they found themselves inside the lobby of a downtown building they did not recognize.

With their mind on one thing only, getting back to their son, both Steven and Fran left through the exit door that was right in front of them.

Chapter 4

After exiting the building, Steven and Fran looked around to get their bearings. They appeared to be outside the old Kingston Hotel. They knew the mountains were to the east, and they needed to head east to return to the apartment complex where Justin was. This was going to be a long journey on foot, at least five miles, and they began the long walk to the East.

It was so unusual not to see anybody on the streets, or any cars on the roads. After making their way out of the downtown area and as far as the interstate interchange, both Steven and Fran were getting tired. Fran stopped and sat down under one of the overpasses.

Steven looked at Fran and said, "We have to keep going."

Fran just replied, "In a minute."

After a few minutes, they continued their journey. Steven knew that the arroyo that ran parallel to the interstate on its north side would eventually veer slightly to the north and continue east. It was built to funnel the spring runoff from the mountains through the city. It was the strangest thing to cross the interstate to reach the arroyo. The interstate was desolate, not a car to be seen in either direction. After reaching the other side, they began following the arroyo along the top, heading east. They knew they would be at risk of being seen, or walking along the bottom of the arroyo, risking death if there would be a sudden raging river of water from out of nowhere, typical of the city's arroyos. Looking up at the sky, and not seeing any sign of impending rainfall, Steven and Fran chose to walk the bottom of the arroyo, in what could be a very deadly decision on their part.

After what seemed to have been about a two-mile walk, Steven and Fran saw a flash in the sky in front of them. Steven knew that flash well, and looking behind, saw a line of clouds rolling in fast from the west. Knowing the risk of impending danger, they headed up the side of the arroyo to the top, once again in danger of being seen, but at least not of losing their lives from a sudden, unexpected torrent of raging water.

At the top of the arroyo, Steven and Fran discovered they were somewhere in the middle of a residential neighborhood. Steven guessed possibly about halfway through their journey. They took their chances walking through someone's driveway, only to discover a running patrol car at the side of the road. The officer was talking to someone who was on the steps of his house, forcefully instructing him to get back inside and stay inside. The officer was standing on the residents lawn with his back turned to Steven and Fran. Steven saw an opportunity and looked at Fran while pointing to the patrol car. They quietly made their way to the driver's side of the patrol car, bending down out of sight. They carefully opened the front and rear doors, with Steven getting in the driver's seat, and Fran directly behind him. Steven floored it, and the roaring sound of the engine alerted the officer, in no uncertain terms, that his car had just been stolen.

Chapter 5

Meanwhile, back at the apartment, Justin had long since quit reading, turned on the TV, and was watching an episode of Interns, frustrated by the constant interruptions instructing residents of the city to stay inside their homes. Six hours had past since Steven and Fran had left for breakfast, and Justin decided to take it upon himself to go searching for his parents. He left the apartment, leaving the door unlocked. He began to walk up the sidewalk, alongside Monterey Boulevard. Upon reaching the stoplight at Monterey and Trolens, he headed south on the bike path that ran alongside Trolens Boulevard.

Completely oblivious to the fact that there were no cars on the road or people on the bike path, he continued heading south alongside Trolens. He intended to ask someone where the Waffle Haven was, but there was no one to be found. Not knowing what else to do, he continued walking, light after light. He eventually found himself at that same intersection his parents were just six hours earlier, but he did not look to the right to see the Waffle Haven a few hundred feet down Centers Avenue. Instead, he crossed the street and continued south on Trolens, which veered to the left after crossing Centers, and stopped at Three Mills Road. The road across Three Mills Road led into a residential neighborhood, and Justin decided to cross the road into the neighborhood.

***

While Justin continued on his impromptu field trip, Steven and Fran were arriving at the apartment complex in their recently acquired patrol car.

They walked down the steps to the apartment door, and opened it yelling, "Justin! Justin!"

A quick search of the apartment revealed that Justin was not there: not in the bathroom, bedrooms, kitchen, or living room, just not there. Now Fran was really worried. Steven told her that everything was going to be alright. They knocked on the neighbor's door, but there was no answer. They knocked on another apartment door, and still no answer.

Fran said, "What's going on, Steven?"

Steven replied, "People are just scared, Fran."

"We've got to find him."

"I know, babe. We'll find him."

Chapter 6

Steven and Fran ditched the patrol car and decided to look for Justin on foot. They walked south on Monterey, toward Justin's high school, and when they got to the school, which was just two lights down, they tried locked door after locked door. About to give up on the school, in desperation, Steven tried one more door. This one opened. Steven and Fran entered and found themselves in an empty classroom. They both made their way to the door on the other side, which opened into a hallway, and they headed down it. The school was desolate, and, as if this wasn't eerie enough, Steven and Fran felt something strange, like a sixth sense telling them they were not alone. They continued walking down the hallway, but the feeling grew stronger. It was as if someone else were there with them. The hallway intersected with another, and they decided to go to the right. Just after beginning to walk down this hallway, Steven looked behind him and caught a glimpse of someone crossing the intersection.

Steven said, "Fran, there's someone else here."

Fran said, "Let's get out of here."

"No, maybe he can help us."

Steven grabbed Fran's hand to lead her back down the hall.

Fran said, "Babe, I don't know about this."

She reluctantly came along, not having much of a choice. Steven followed the man down the hallway, with Fran at his side. First at a distance, but then the man began to walk faster, so Steven kept pace, with Fran right behind him. As Steven got closer, he could see that the man was wearing an old army jacket, paired with blue jeans and no shoes. He was a thin man with long brown hair that looked like it had not been cared for. Realizing he was being followed, the man began to run. Steven ran after him.

Fran yelled, "Steven, no!!"

Steven did not heed her warning, and he continued to run after the man. The man ran down the hallway, but the hallway ended at a set of exit doors that were locked.

Catching up with the man, Steven asked him, "Who are you? And what are you doing here?"

The man, who looked at Steven in an almost sheepish fashion, said, "I heard the police cars' warnings, and I didn't have anywhere to go."

"How did you get in here?"

"The same way you did, through the open door."

Steven asked the man if he saw anyone else in the school, and the man said he hadn't.

Fran looked at Steven and said, "We have to, Steven. We have to find him."

As Steven and Fran turned to leave, the man yelled, "You can't go out there! It's not safe!"

Steven and Fran made their way back the way they came, and as they left, Fran suggested they try Holoman's Fun Center on Trolens. This was going to be a long walk, but they knew Justin was on foot. They headed south on John Taylor Boulevard, and after the long walk four lights down John Taylor, they headed east on Old School Street. After crossing Hyland Park Street, they continued east to Holoman's Fun Center on the corner of Trolens and Old School.

Steven and Fran had intended to look in the arcade and laser tag building, but the doors were locked. There were employees inside, but they yelled that they were instructed not to open the doors until told otherwise. They also told Steven and Fran that they should be indoors. They tried the other arcade across the parking lot, but they were met with the same fate.

Steven and Fran were exhausted, disillusioned, and felt

they were out of options, but they also felt they had to press on. They sat on the steps to rest, regroup, and plan their next move.

After spending some time resting, Fran said to Steven, "Maybe he decided to go look for us."

Steven replied, "Maybe, he knew we were going to breakfast."

They decided to head south on Trolens, towards Waffle Haven. After another long, agonizing walk south on Trolens, through light after light, Steven and Fran found themselves at the very same intersection where this whole ordeal started earlier this morning.

Steven started to head west on the sidewalk along Centers. It was starting to get dark now.

Fran said to Steven, "Wait, Steven. Justin wouldn't have gone down there. I know him. He doesn't think. He would've just crossed the street."

Steven replied, "How do you know that?"

Fran just stared at Steven and said, "Think about it, Steven."

"Yeah, you're right."

They crossed Centers and continued south on Trolens, which veered to the left now and stopped at Three Mills. It was starting to get very dark when Steven and Fran made it to the intersection of Trolens and Three Mills. The road across Three Mills led into a residential neighborhood.

Fran saw someone across the street and yelled, "Hey!"

The voice from across the street replied, "Hey, what?"

At that moment, Fran knew it was Justin.

Chapter 7

After crossing the street to meet Justin, Fran said to him, "What were you thinking?"

"I was looking for you," replied Justin.

Steven said, "Justin, we've been searching for hours for you. Why didn't you stay at the apartment like they said to on the TV?"

"I didn't hear that part. I was watching Interns."

"How could you not hear that part? It was on every..." Steven replied, but stopped his sentence short, remembering the past sixteen years and knowing what Justin's response should be. "Never mind," he said.

Fran said, "Let's go home."

To that, Steven said, "We can't go home. They're going to be looking for us."

"What are we going to do, Steven?" There was a slight pause, then Fran said, "Here's what I think we should do. First, we need to get rid of the police car. Then I think we should stay at the neighbor's and lie low for a while."

"Fran, if the neighbors didn't answer the door the first time, they're not going to now. Besides, by now the cops are going to be crawling all over that patrol car."

"I don't think so. I think most of them are inside."

"So what do you want to do, Fran?"

"I think we should find a place to hold up inside and lie low for a while."

"Where do you want to go?"

"I don't know. Somewhere safe and where they won't be looking for us."

"There's an old motel on Centers. We can head down there and stay there for a while."

So Fran, Justin, and Steven began to walk down Centers, this time heading down an alley that ran parallel with the road. It wasn't very long until they came upon the old Route 77 Motel and Diner. The door in the rear had a padlock on it, but there was a partially broken window just to the left. Steven picked up an old board that was lying on the ground and broke the window the rest of the way.

Looking at Fran, he said, "Let's go."

Fran said, "I don't want to do this, Babe."

"We have to."

After all three of them made their way inside, they found themselves in a motel room. The room was dirty and had one king bed with a nightstand and lamp on each side.

Fran felt something brush against her ankle in the dark and said, "Oh my God! What was that?"

"Probably a rat," Steven replied.

"Let's get out of here."

"We can't. It's dark. Besides, it's just one night."

At that moment, Justin said, "I'm tired. I'm going to bed," and proceeded to crawl up and lie down on the bed in the room.

"Just a minute, Justin," Steven said.

Steven found the door to the room, which opened up into a darkened hallway.

After opening the door just across the hallway, Steven discovered a room that had two beds, and he said, "Over here, guys."

Fran and Justin made their way over and settled into bed for the night. The next morning, it dawned on Steven that after hours of all three of them being outside, they all felt fine.

Steven told Fran, "I don't think there is any airborne virus."

"What makes you say that?" asked Fran.

"All three of us have been out for hours, and we're all fine."

"So what do we do?"

"We can't keep walking. We have got to get someone else with a car to realize there is no danger. Then, somehow, we've got to convince everyone else there is no danger."

"How are we going to do that?"

"I don't know. You got any ideas?"

"I think we should go to the news media."

"You're right, Fran, but there are people looking for us right now."

"What are you suggesting?"

"We need to get out of the city. We should head east, find a small town, and lie low for a while."

"We need a car."

"Over there," Justin said while pointing across the street to the many used car lots along Centers Boulevard.

Steven said, "Justin, you're a genius."

After crossing the street, Steven, Justin, and Fran began to look for a car with a key in it. It didn't take long before Justin blurted out, "I found one!"

Steven got in the driver's seat, Fran in the front passenger's seat, and Justin behind Steven. The car was an early 2000 model, silver, four-door sedan. Fortunately, there was about a quarter tank of fuel, and Steven figured that would safely get him out of the city before stopping at the next gas station. They headed east out of the city and, by some miracle, did not run into any patrol cars. As Steven approached the on-ramp to the freeway, he saw a metal gate blocking it and went through the grass around the left side of it.

As they traveled east on the interstate, through the pass, there were no cars to be seen. At the top of the hill, on the other side of the pass, there was a convenience store. Steven knew if he used his credit card to get gas, the Law would know where they were, but he didn't have a choice. He looked around, put his card in the pump, punched in the zip code, and started pumping. He had intended to fill the tank, but the longer he pumped, the more uneasy he felt. Looking over his shoulder, he saw a curtain move in the double-wide trailer just behind and above the station. He heard glass shatter, and he knew what that meant. He pulled the hose from the car, hung it up, and ran to the driver's side. Just as he got in, he heard what sounded like a firecracker, and he gunned it and headed back onto the interstate. The gas gauge now showed three quarters of a tank.

About seventy miles out of the city, Steven turned north onto Route 7, which led up into the mountains, and to the tiny town of Bellenova. There were no stores or gas stations there, just a couple of houses in the middle of nowhere in the mountains. Steven turned down a small dirt driveway, not knowing where it would lead. The driveway ended in a meadow surrounded by trees. It was still early in the day, but Steven and Fran both felt they needed to stay here for the night.

Chapter 8

The next morning, Steven, Fran, and Justin headed north on Route 7 again. This took them to another interstate that ran north and south through the state. This interstate actually took a slight jog to the East before continuing north, though. Steven turned onto the interstate with the intention of heading toward the town of Vincent, a small college town in the northern part of the state, but still large enough to have a TV station, though be it a college station. As he headed north on the interstate, the first thing Steven noticed was that there were now cars traveling in both directions, though sparse. As he drew closer to town, traffic became heavier, and Steven and Fran both began worrying about being seen. They exited the freeway at the first opportunity.

Steven looked for a large parking lot, but there were none to be found. He decided to ditch the car in a vacant lot behind two buildings on a side street. Fran and Steven both knew that there would be people looking for them, and they also knew that all three of them needed to change their look. Planning to do just that, they headed for the college.

Fortunately, the college was on the South side of the town, and it wouldn't be too far on foot. After a half-mile walk to the North, Steven, Fran, and Justin could see the campus buildings in the East. Walking on campus, they didn't quite blend in with the other students, but they also weren't the object of anyone's attention. After a short period of time, Steven thought it would be safe to ask one of the students where the Cosmetology department was. A young, man in his mid-twenties wearing blue jeans and a T-shirt, pointed to the

East and said it was two buildings beyond the one directly in front of them, and there would be a department directory just inside the entrance.

When the three entered the building, there was a hallway directly in front of them, and one to the left. Looking on the wall to the left of him, Steven saw the department directory the young man told him about. It stated that the Cosmetology lab was two doors down on the left in the hallway directly in front of them. When they entered the room, to the right of them was a counter. The room was set up like a beauty salon, only larger.

A young lady, probably in her early twenties, came up to the counter and asked, "Can I help you?"

Steven asked how much for a haircut, and the young lady replied that it was $7.50, which was about half the price in a chain hair salon. He also asked what they would charge to color Fran's hair, and the young lady said it was $40.00, again about half the price of what it would be in a chain salon. Looking in his wallet, Steven saw he had about $125.00. He had always tried to stretch a dollar.

Knowing this, Fran looked at him, and said, "You know we have to do this."

Steven and Justin both had their hair cut, and Fran died her hair black, a far cry from the blonde it was, yet, black was her natural color.

Chapter 9

Steven and Fran wanted to know what was really going on in Chartersville, and they had every intention of finding out. Knowing that Vincent's one TV station was located right here, at the college, Steven asked another student where to find it. Once they had directions, Steven, Fran, and Justin headed to the TV station. As they approached the building, there was a plaque to the right of the door that read:

"Norton Blackwell Building"

"Media Arts Center"

"1969".

Upon entering, once again there was a hallway directly in front of them, and one to the left of them. On the wall to the right was a directory. Reading the directory, Steven determined that the TV station they were looking for was down the hall in front of them and through the third door on the left. This room was small and had a counter to the right and a seating area to the left. There was a young girl, in her early twenties, behind the counter.

As the three entered, the young girl asked, "May I help you?"

Steven asked to see a reporter, and the young lady replied that the reporters were on assignments. She asked if there was anything she could help them with.

Steven replied, "We really need to see a reporter."

The young lady replied, "You're welcome to wait. However, I'm not sure when they will be returning to the studio."

Steven and Fran decided to wait, knowing that it would

be safer for them to stay indoors for a while and taking advantage of a much needed opportunity to rest. Two hours must have passed by, and the door to the room opened.

A young man, in his early twenties, walked in, and the girl behind the counter said, "John, these people are waiting for you."

Looking to the left, at Steven and Fran, the young man asked, "May I help you?"

Steven introduced himself, saying, "Hi. I'm Steven. This is my wife Fran, and my son Justin. We wanted to talk to you about the situation in Chartersville."

"We're well aware of the bio-hazard threat to Chartersville. We've been told that it is not going to affect us here in Vincent."

"I think there is more to it than that."

John replied, "Come with me," motioning for Steven, Fran, and Justin to follow him down a small corridor on the right, pass the counter.

There were two doors on the right, and John's office was the second.

As they entered the small office, John walked behind his desk and said to the three, "Have a seat."

Justin remained standing, as there were only two seats.

After that, John sat down and asked, "What can you tell me?"

After about forty-five minutes of Steven, Fran, and even Justin, relaying to John all of the events that had taken place in the last three days, John's replied, "Nothing you've told me would lead me to believe the situation in Chartersville is anything more than what we've been told."

Frustrated, Steven asked if there was anyone else they could talk to.

John replied, "Look, we only have one other reporter. He's not here right now, and I'm certain he would agree with me."

Not knowing where to go or what to do next, Steven, Fran, and Justin left the studio. As they were walking down the hallway to leave the building, a young man wearing a blue suit noticed that the three seemed out of place for the college and asked if he could help them find anything.

Steven replied, "No, we already tried, and no one will believe us anyway."

"Believe what?" the young man asked.

"It doesn't matter," a comment Steven only said out of frustration.

"Look, my name is Tony Barton. I'm an anchor here at KCBY. If you decide you want to tell me, give me a call," the young man said, as he handed Steven a business card.

Steven, Fran, and Justin left the college having no idea where they would stay that evening. They thought it best to head south from the college, away from town, as there would be less chance of people noticing them. They came across an old, vacant outbuilding that appeared to be on the outskirts of someone's ranch. This would at least afford them some protection from the weather, and they decided to stay here for the evening. As it started to get dark, they could see lighting flashes in the sky and heard thunder in the distance. Steven knew this was going to be a long night, as Fran was deathly afraid of thunderstorms. As all three settled in for the night, in an attempt to get some sleep, the lighting flashes increased, and the thunder just got louder. It wasn't too much longer before the first drops of rain started to come through what once was a roof. Fran just lied there, wide awake, curled up in a fetal position as Steven tried to comfort her. Nothing he could say this time would make the situation they were in any easier. As time passed, Steven knew Fran was still awake as he held her. Fran looked a few feet over and saw Justin fast asleep and snoring as the raindrops fell onto his jeans and T-shirt.

Chapter 10

The next morning, the first words out of Fran's mouth were, "I'm not going to do this anymore! I'm tired. I'm cold. I'm wet. I'm just not going to do this anymore!"

Steven replied, "What are we supposed to do, Fran? We can't go back to Chartersville. No one will listen to us."

"Let's go talk to that Tony guy."

"What good will that do? No one listened to a thing we said anyway."

"Let's just try."

They headed back to the college and to the Media Arts building they were in.

When they entered the studio, Steven asked, "Is Tony Barton here?"

The young lady behind the counter replied, "Yes he is, and you're in luck. He's not on the air. Who should I say is here to see him?"

"My name is Steven. He will know who I am. We've talked before."

Shortly thereafter, Tony came into the lobby from the hall and, upon seeing Steven, Fran, and Justin sitting down in the chairs provided, he said, "Steven, what can I do for you?"

This time, after being escorted to the first door on the right, Steven, Fran, and Justin again found themselves in a small office. Steven and Fran sat down in the two seats provided, and Justin found himself standing once again. The three relayed the same story to Tony, just as they told to John before. This time the reaction was different.

Tony said, "If your suspicions are right, I'm very

interested in your story." He continued, "I'd like to take the opportunity to dig into this some more. I'll let you know what I find out. Where are you staying?"

Steven replied, "We're not staying anywhere at the moment."

"Look, my mom has an efficiency apartment above her garage. Let me talk to her, and we'll see what we can do. For now, my roommate is just going to have to deal with you three staying with us. Come on, I'll give you a ride."

Tony led all three of them out of the Media Arts building to an adjacent parking lot. His vehicle was a late-model, silver sedan, and Fran got into the passenger's seat, while Steven and Justin got in the back. On the short drive over to Tony's place, the silence was rather awkward, so, just to break the ice, Fran asked Tony if he had any family. Tony replied that he had two brothers and a sister, and all of them lived out of state. It was only a few minutes before they pulled up alongside a duplex on the right side of the street. It was a flat-roofed, stucco building, with a metal roll-up garage door on each side, and an entrance to the right of the garage door on the left. On the other side, the entrance was to the left, and the center had two windows next to each other. Tony's place was on the left.

Surprisingly, Tony pulled out a key and said, "Here, this is an extra key. I already let my roommate know that you might be staying with us for a few days."

Steven felt slightly uncomfortable as he turned the key to enter the duplex, although this couldn't be any worse than anything they had done in the last few days. As they entered, there was a combined kitchen and dining area to the right, and the living room was directly in front of them. There was a hallway to the left that led to a bedroom on each side, toward the back of the house. Still exhausted, Fran immediately made her way to the couch in the living room, where she promptly lied down. Justin followed suit and headed to one of the back bedrooms with no qualms about falling asleep on someone else's bed. Uncomfortable about being in another strange place,

Steven decided to stay awake and pulled up a dining chair next to the TV and turned it on with the volume rather low.

After a couple of hours, a key turned in the door, and a young man, in his early twenties, walked through.

He looked at Steven and said, "Hi, I'm Frank. Tony told me that you might be staying here for a little while."

Steven introduced himself, and the two talked for a while as Fran and Justin slept. Steven once again relayed their story to Frank.

Afterward, Frank replied, "Well, if there's anybody who can get to the bottom of a story, it's Tony."

Steven and Frank continued to talk for a while, and, eventually, the front door opened again. This time it was Tony. He had two big bags with him, one in each hand. As he entered and shut the door behind him, he asked if anyone was hungry.

Frank replied, "I sure am, and I'm sure these three are, too."

Tony just said, "Well there's plenty." He pulled out two boxes of chicken, two one-pound containers of coleslaw, and a box of eight biscuits.

Steven knew Fran would be in heaven right about now, so he gently woke her up. All of them enjoyed the food, and for the first time in a while, Fran had a sense that things were about to get better.

Tony looked at Steven and said, "I talked to my mom, and it took some convincing, but she agreed to let you stay in the efficiency. The only catch is, you have to do some odd-jobs around the house." He continued, "Ever since Dad died, she hasn't had the time or energy to keep things up."

Steven looked at this as an opportunity to stay out of sight, and he gladly accepted the opportunity.

Chapter 11

The next day, Tony took Steven, Fran, and Justin over to his mom's house on his way to the college. He walked up to the house in front of Steven, Fran, and Justin and rang the doorbell.

A woman in her mid-forties answered the doorbell and opened the screen door while saying, "Hi, Tony. This must be the three you were talking about." The woman introduced herself, saying, "Hi, I'm Sarah. You must be the three Tony was telling me about."

Steven gently shook her hand and said, "Hi, I'm Steven."

Fran followed him with a hearty, "Hi, I'm Fran." In that sheepish yet very sincere voice, she added "And this is my son, Justin."

The house was a large, single-story ranch, and the two-story garage in front of it looked rather out of place.

The five of them talked for a while, and Tony finally said, "Well, I have to get to the college. Mom will take care of you."

As Tony left, Sarah said, "Well, I'm sure you're anxious to get settled in," and the four of them walked over to the garage.

They entered through a door on the side of the garage, and, immediately on the right, inside the garage, there was a wooden stairway that led up to an open kitchen in the corner. To the left was a bathroom. On the right, just off the kitchen, the next door down was a walk-in closet. The space on the left over the garage was one room furnished with a sleeper sofa and two end tables on the left wall. There was a computer desk with a chair, and a nineteen-inch TV and stand on the opposite wall.

Sarah said, "It's not much, but it's all we have."

"It will do just fine," Steven said.

"I'll see if I have an air mattress for the young one."

Fran and Justin looked around, and shortly thereafter, Sarah came back up the stairs with a box that contained an air mattress and a pump. She told Fran that there was some bedding in the closet.

Sarah then said, "Steven, I have something for you," as she handed him an envelope.

Sarah walked back down the stairs, and Steven looked at Fran as he held the envelope.

"Well, open it," Fran said.

Steven pulled out three sheets of notebook paper that contained a rather long list of things that needed to be done around the house.

"Well, what is it?" Fran asked.

"It's a list of chores," Steven replied.

"Well, what are they?"

Steven began to read aloud the things on the list. About halfway down, it read: "Remove hornets nest from shed in backyard." He had no idea how he was going to do this, as he was deathly afraid of any type of bee, let alone hornets. He knew that in order to accomplish the rest of tasks on the list, though, he would have to get rid of the hornets first. He set out to find wasp and hornet killer and was successful at locating two cans in the garage below, though one was half empty. He headed for the backyard, armed with the two cans of wasp and hornet spray. He felt apprehension as he entered the backyard; however, he knew he had to turn these feelings into determination if he was to be successful. Stopping about halfway through the backyard, Steven shook the full can well. He could see the hornets hovering around the top of the nest and heard a very faint hum in the distance. He shot a stream from the can away from the nest to test the distance. Now that he was confident the can would reach the nest, he aimed it directly at the nest and soaked it with the entire can. He could see some hornets fall to the ground as a few others flew away, probably to their deaths.

Once the can was exhausted, Steven headed back to the apartment above the garage to regroup before returning to douse the nest with the remaining hornet and wasp spray in the other can. Once he got his bearings again, he returned to the backyard and exhausted the remaining can on the nest. He explained to Tony's mother that it would be best if they waited until tomorrow before removing the nest, and as a result, some of the other chores would have to wait. She agreed, and Steven worked on some of the simpler chores in the front of the house, well aware that mowing the lawn should not be one of them.

Later that evening, Steven returned to the apartment above the garage again and found Fran cooking something on the stove. It seemed the pantry was very well stocked and a can of potatoes, a can of sliced carrots, and two cans of beef made a very hearty stew. The three ate dinner and settled down to watch TV afterward, before going to bed. It was so nice to have some element of home and actually feel safe as they went to sleep for the evening.

The next day, Tony stopped by, after a long day at the college. He came to see Steven and Fran.

Sitting on the sofa in the apartment above the garage, Tony said to Steven, "Remember when I told you I would let you know what I find out about the situation in Chartersville?"

Steven replied, "Yeah."

"Well, we sent one of our reporters to Chartersville to follow up on what you told us. Getting into the city was difficult, but we managed to do it. Not only did we manage to do that, but we succeeded in our quest to talk to a few of the residents. It seems none of the people we talked to have any symptoms whatsoever, except cabin fever. You guys just stay here and lay low for a while, and in the meantime, we're going to really dig in and get all the facts before we break this story."

So Steven continued to do the odd-jobs that Sarah

requested, although it really wasn't what he was used to. On the other hand, Fran was starting to feel comfortable with her surroundings, and Justin would be happy anywhere.

Chapter 12

Steven knew that, for the moment, staying where they were at was probably the best thing, but eventually they would have to leave, so they decided to stay and do as Tony asked. The next day, Steven continued working on the list Sarah had asked him to do. After cleaning the apartment, Fran settled down with a good book. Justin found an older model video game player and a few games along with it in the closet. He immediately hooked it up to the TV with no trouble at all. That was one of the things he was good at. Two days passed with basically the same routine in place.

This was the fifth day in the apartment, and around mid-afternoon, Tony showed up while Steven was mowing the Lawn.

With the car still running, Tony motioned to Steven to cut the lawnmower's engine and yelled out the window, "Steven, get Fran and Justin. We've got to get out of here now!"

Steven ran upstairs to the apartment and told Fran, "We've got to go."

Fran replied, "But I'm in the middle of the best part," referring to the book she was reading.

Steven replied with a more stern voice, "Fran, we've got to go now!"

Fran looked at Justin and said, "Justin, turn the TV off, we have to go."

Justin responded, "But I'm almost at the next level."

"Turn the TV off. We have to go now."

Steven, Fran, and Justin all headed downstairs and outside to Tony's car.

As soon as they got in, Tony took off and said, "What took you so long? We've got to get you out of here. I know a place near the college you can stay."

"What's going on?" asked Steven.

"We broke the story in Chartersville. I'm going on the air in less than thirty minutes."

As they drove the short drive to the college, they passed by the two buildings in front of the vacant lot where Steven and Fran had ditched the car they were driving when they first arrived in Vincent. On each side of the building, there were patrol cars. It was just a couple of minutes before Tony pulled up to a small adobe style house with a flat roof.

Tony said, "This is Kendra's house, the young lady you met behind the receptionist desk at the station. She's not there right now, but she lives with her mother. You can stay here right now. Her mother knows you're coming."

As Steven, Fran, and Justin got out and shut the car doors, Tony took off down the street like he was on his way to a fire. Apprehensively, Steven, Fran, and Justin walked up to the door of the house and rang the doorbell. A lady in her mid-forties answered the door.

She looked at the three of them and said, as she opened the door, "You must be the three Tony was telling me about. Come on in."

It was slightly dark in the house, and Steven's eyes took a minute to adjust to the room's light level, as it was very bright outside. The furniture was older, with a flowery couch and a couple of pole lamps on each end. There was a matching chair and coffee table in front of the couch. On the opposite wall was a console TV with a converter box on top of it. The TV was on and set to the college station.

The lady that had invited them in said, "Oh my word, I haven't even introduced myself. I'm Charolette, Kendra's mother. Have a seat. Would you like anything to drink?"

"Just some water," Steven said as all three of them sat down.

Mowing the lawn in the hot weather, the ride over, and

the anxiety of not knowing what was going to happen next necessitated the water.

"Nothing for me," Fran said.

"Do you have any soda?" Justin blurted out in his usual straight-forward way.

As Charolette brought back Steven's water and Justin's root beer, she said, "Tony told me to put the college station on and leave it there. He's about to go on the air. I don't quite understand because the college news doesn't usually come on until 4:00 PM."

Shortly after that, all three of them were sitting down watching the TV. There was a show on that was explaining the difference in the minerals found in different types of rocks. The show was interrupted, and Tony appeared onscreen, wearing what appeared to be the same blue suit he was wearing when the three first met him.

Tony began to speak, "We are interrupting our broadcast of Geology 101 with an important news update. KCBY has recently learned that the bio-hazard threat in Chartersville does not exist. We take you now to an undisclosed location in Chartersville, where reporter John Sogon is live with a special report."

Next on the screen appeared the man who didn't believe what Steven and Fran told him in the first place.

He began, "Thanks, Tony. I'm here in Chartersville, where we've recently learned that the bio-hazard threat previously reported was erroneous. KCBY has learned from a reliable source that John Clemens, the city's bio-hazard safety director, was directed by a federal agency, currently unnamed, to establish the bio-hazard threat story in an effort to quarantine the city. At this point, authorities are still mandating that no one is allowed in or out of the city. Our source believes that the quarantine project was initiated by the Office of National Protection, with the intention of using Chartersville as an experiment to see if a national quarantine could be implemented without creating civil unrest, although, at this point, that cannot be confirmed. As we learn more we will keep you updated. I'm John Sogon, reporting for KCBY news."

Tony reappeared back on screen and said, "Thanks John." He continued, "KCBY news will keep you updated as this story develops. We now return you to Geology 101."

As the geology show returned to the TV screen, Charolette said, "Oh my God! I can't believe this!"

Steven replied, "Neither can I. They're going to be looking for us."

Fran asked, "But why us?"

"Think about it, Fran. We're the only ones who made it out of the city. If that fact comes out, someone in that unnamed federal agency is not going to be a happy camper."

It wasn't but thirty minutes when there was a knock at the front door. Charolette answered the door, and it was Tony.

He asked Steven, "Did you see our news broadcast?"

Steven replied, "Yeah, we saw it."

"You know you can't stay here."

"I know."

"Steven, there's more." There was a slight pause, and Tony continued, "While we were reporting our exclusive, at the same time, the three major networks were flashing your and Fran's pictures with some bogus story about you two escaping from two different medium security prisons in the western part of the state. They said you two may be traveling with a sixteen-year-old male and showed a composite sketch of Justin."

Fran said, "But what about Josh?"

"Who's Josh?"

"My other son. He lives with his grandmother in Trade City."

"You can't go there. That's the first place they'll look."

"What are we going to do, Steven?"

Tony looked at Fran and said, "Look, as soon as things calm down a bit in Chartersville, we'll get word to your family in Trade City that you three are on the run."

Fran immediately asked, "What do you mean 'on the run'?"

Steven looked at Fran and said, "I'm sorry all this

happened, but now we have to deal with it."

Fran looked at Steven and said, "None of this would've happened if you didn't take me to breakfast."

"You're the one who wanted to go out."

Tony replied, "OK, you guys, I'm sorry, but you gotta go."

Steven and Fran knew that the three of them had to leave town, and fast, without being discovered. By now, after stealing two cars, Steven thought a third one wouldn't really matter, but he was no professional car thief. The three of them started walking towards town. They knew they were taking a risk, but they were hoping to find a car someone left running. As they approached town, there was a convenience on the first main street they came across. With some luck, they continued to the next convenience store just down the street. This one had a compact car pulled up along the side of the building. By some miracle, the driver was dumb enough to leave it running as he popped into the store. Apparently, he didn't anticipate the long line, and that gave Steven, Fran, and Justin the perfect opportunity.

Steven yelled to Justin, "Get in," as they approached the car.

Justin just looked at Steven with a blank look on his face.

Steven repeated louder, "Justin, get in!"

Justin complied as the three of them jumped in the car and Steven tore out of the parking lot. As he looked in the mirror, he saw a man run out the store and throw his coffee cup toward the back of the car. Steven knew he had to stay off the interstates, so he headed north out of town on Route 216 toward the tiny town of Ronkers. From there, there was a dirt road that continued north through a national forest, not the kind of road you would expect a small compact car on, and that was exactly what Steven wanted.

As he drove the dirt road, there were several smaller dirt roads that led off it. He chose one that led off to the left. As they descended down what appeared to be a small dirt driveway, the rocks became larger and the ruts deeper.

Fran said, "What are you doing? You can't go down there!"

Steven replied, "Watch me."

He carefully maneuvered the car around the rocks, while straddling the ruts. After what seemed like several miles, but probably was no more than half a mile, he turned off to the right on another driveway that led downward, hiding the car from the road above.

Steven said, "Let's stay here a few days until things cool off."

Fran just replied, "Whatever you want," in a frustrated tone.

Steven looked in the trunk in hopes of finding something he could use. Inside the trunk, he found a rope, some tools, and a winter kit. The winter kit had a label on the outside that read "Five Person Deluxe Survival Kit".

As Steven read the contents listed on the label, he said, "We hit the jackpot, Fran."

The kit contained just about everything they needed for a short stay in the mountains, away from civilization: food, a small tent, light sticks, matches, a first aid kit, a makeshift toilet, a hand-crank radio, and more, including a manual on how to use it all. Steven set about setting up camp, while Fran found a nearby rock she could sit down on and retreat into reading one of her romance novels. Normally Steven would ask Fran to help him and receive the usual reply, "What do you need help with?" offered up in exchange for the real question she was thinking to herself, which was "Why can't you do it yourself?" However, Steven knew how frustrated Fran was and thought better than even asking this time. In about an hour, he had a makeshift camp set up, which would be their temporary home for a couple of days.

After camp was set up, Justin said he was tired and decided to take a nap in the tent. The surface of the tent floor was slightly rocky, but Justin could sleep anywhere. Steven knew that when it was time for himself and Fran to turn in for the night, Fran was not going to be quite so content. As Fran continued to read her book, Steven decided to crank up the radio.

As soon as Steven cranked up the radio and tuned it to a station that had a clear signal, he heard these words, "Civil unrest continues in Chartersville as authorities struggle to maintain the peace. The chaos in Chartersville erupted after a small college TV station in Vincent broke the story that the bio-hazard threat in Chartersville did not exist and was actually a ploy to keep the city in a quarantine state as part of an experiment by a federal agency, ironically, to see if a city the size of Chartersville could be quarantined without civil unrest. Meanwhile, authorities continue their search for two prisoners that escaped from two different medium-security prisons in the western part of the state: Steven Fruskin and Fran Fruskin, both in their mid-forties and believed to be traveling with a sixteen-year-old male. They were last seen leaving a convenience store in a stolen compact car in the small college town of Vincent. The vehicle is described as a silver, 2007, Nissan Sentra, four-door, with New Mexico plates KCB 927. If you see this vehicle, authorities are requesting that you do not approach the vehicle, instead, immediately contact local authorities. In other news, a new manufacturing facility has recently announced their intentions of possibly locating in Chartersville. If Chartersville is chosen, the facility would employ approximately 250 people. And now, another full hour of commercial free music on your number one station for country favorites, KNRT."

With that, Steven shut off the radio and told Fran that he was going to look around a bit. Fran continued to read her book as Steven set out to become a little more familiar with his surroundings.

After a short while, Steven returned to the camp and told Fran, "It looks like we're pretty isolated down here."

Fran just replied with, "I'm hungry."

Steven opened the cars trunk, pulled out one of the energy bars from the survival kit, and handed it to Fran.

Surprisingly, the energy bar was rather filling and Fran was satisfied. As night fell, Steven and Fran retired to the tent, where Justin had been sleeping the whole time. Amazingly, Fran offered no complaints about the rocky ground and immediately fell asleep. This time it was Steven who couldn't sleep. He was thinking about all that had transpired, what he was going to do to make this right, and how he was going to restore their lives to some sort of normalcy. Although slowly, night passed, and as dawn approached, Steven was the first one out of the tent. He was thinking to himself what he wouldn't give for a good cup of coffee right now, but instead, settled for an energy bar and water from the survival kit.

Chapter 13

Two more days passed, and Steven thought it safe to leave camp. Fran helped to pack up, and after loading everything back in the trunk of the car, the three of them got in and headed out of the forest. Steven still thought it best to stay off the major highways, so he continued north on the dirt road he had originally turned off of.

After a couple of hours of driving, the three of them found themselves in yet another small town, this time in south-central Colorado. Not wanting to draw attention to the three of them, and with still half a tank of gas, Steven decided to continue traveling north through the town. He knew that the authorities would be looking for the vehicle they were in, and they needed to find another form of transportation, albeit, an inconspicuous one. Reaching the tiny town of Fort Brazen, Colorado, Steven, Fran, and Justin left the car hidden over an embankment on the side of the road and continued northeast on foot.

After walking for about three-quarters of a mile, they came across some railroad tracks. The tracks ran up an incline toward the mountain pass. Steven knew the train would have to slow down here, and that gave him an idea. All three of them waited near the tracks, out of sight of an oncoming train. It was only about two hours when the freight train appeared from the South. The train was already slowing due to the long incline. There were freight cars, tanker cars, coal cars, flat cars, and several freight cars had the doors open.

Steven explained to Fran and Justin what they had to do, and as the train approached, it began to slow to a crawl.

Surprisingly, the train came to a complete stop. Steven seized the opportunity and climbed up in one of the open box cars. He grabbed Fran's arms and managed to pull her up. Once the two of them were in the box car, they both helped pull up Justin, and the three of them headed toward the back of the car.

The box car was empty, except for a bed of straw, and it smelled musty. They all had no idea what was in it previously, but they were all glad it was empty. After about thirty minutes, the train began to move again, though slowly. The train began its ascent north, toward the pass, and Steven, Fran, and Justin settled in for the ride. As the train began its journey through the pass, the three of them could see out the doors of the box car, and the view began to look spectacular, the likes of which Steven and Fran had not seen since their passenger train trip up the west coast several years ago.

As the train continued its journey, Fran said to Steven, "I'm cold."

All Steven could do was cuddle up close to Fran to keep her warm. Looking to the right of them, once again, Justin was asleep on the bed of straw. That boy could sleep anywhere.

The train ride continued through the night, and Steven and Fran awoke the next day to find themselves somewhere in the state of Wyoming. They looked to their right and found Justin still sleeping. At this point they were cold and hungry. Even though he didn't know quite where they were, Steven decided it best if the three of them got off the train now, although he wasn't sure how they were going to do that, given the speed the train was traveling. Not wanting to risk injury, Steven decided the three of them should wait a little while longer. Time passed and eventually the train began to slow as it started to ascend up what appeared to be another mountain pass.

After just a few short minutes, the train was moving at a crawl and Steven told Fran and Justin, "This is where we get off."

Steven told Justin that he was going to have to jump, but not to until he was told to do so. Steven also told Justin to stay right where he jumped, and he would come get him. The train was moving even slower now, almost as if it were about to stop.

As soon as Steven saw a spot level enough, he yelled, "Jump, Justin! Jump!"

"I don't think so, Dad," replied Justin.

"Just do it! Do it now!"

Reluctantly, Justin jumped. Steven could see that Justin landed on his lap and slid a little ways.

He looked at Fran and said, "Your turn. I'm right behind you."

Fran replied, "You go first. I'll jump when I'm ready."

Steven jumped and rolled down a slight hill, but he was okay. Fran did not want to jump, but knowing her husband and son did and looking at the rugged terrain to come, it was enough to inspire her to take a leap of faith. Amazingly, Fran landed in the tall grass of the beginning of a meadow that bordered the tracks.

Steven could see Fran from where he landed and headed towards her.

When he was in voice range, he yelled, "We've got to get Justin."

The two met up and followed the tracks back to find Justin. After finding him, amazingly, right where he was told to stay, and thank God none of them were hurt, Steven thought it best that they look for shelter before it was dark. He heard what he thought was the gurgling of a stream, and the three of them headed for the sound. Sure enough, at the bottom of a hill, there was indeed a stream, and a wide one at that.

The three of them followed the river downstream for about two miles before they looked across it and saw a cabin with the windows bordered up on the other side. It was slightly up the hill, overlooking the river with a balcony, and it had stilts in front of it for a foundation. Just downstream, there was a tree that had fallen across the river, and Steven and Fran thought this would make a nice bridge. When they made it to the tree, it was wider than it had looked, and all three of them had no problem crossing.

On the other side, the three of them headed to the cabin they saw and walked around to the other side and found the entryway padlocked. Given their circumstances, Steven rationalized that his family was more important than one more felony. He kicked the door as hard as he could, near the hasp and lock, and the door swung open. Inside, there was a kitchen on the right as you entered, a dining table next to the windows that overlooked the river, a couch, a chair, and a free standing fireplace. There was a small bathroom with a chemical toilet and a makeshift shower, which utilized water from a tank above it. The refrigerator was empty, but there were still canned goods in the cupboard. Most of the cooking utensils had been removed from the cupboard, with the exception of a couple of pots and pans, some tin plates, and a few pieces of flatware. Another cupboard contained an old rag, a bottle of dish soap, and matches.

Steven gathered some wood from around the cabin and built a fire in the fireplace. Fran heated up some canned soup she found in the cupboard. The three of them rested there for the evening. Steven knew they had to keep moving at first light, or risk being found by the law enforcement agencies looking for them. When morning came, the three prepared to leave. Upon opening the cabin door, Steven was greeted by the barrel of a shotgun and a short scraggly looking man with a long beard and an old hat that looked like it was recently purchased from a thrift store.

The man's first words towards Steven were "Don't move."

Steven replied, "We don't mean you any harm."

The man said, "I know you don't. I've got the gun. What are you folks doing here anyway?"

"It's a long story."

"Oh? I've got time because you folks are comin' with me."

He motioned the three out of the cabin with a wave of the shotgun, and they had no choice but to do as they were told.

The man told them to start up a steep trail that led from the cabin up the hill behind it.

Steven asked, "Where are you taking us?"

The man replied, "Why don't you answer my question first? Then I'll think about answering yours."

Steven relayed his story to the man, the whole story. It actually felt good to get it out, almost like some sort of weight had been lifted from him, even though he didn't know what was next.

After hearing Steven's story, the man said, "So you're them folks everybody's been lookin' for. I always thought there was more to it then the news folks were sayin'. So you weren't in no jail?"

"I haven't been in jail a day in my life," replied Steven.

"Well, I'll tell you what. I tend to believe you," the man said as he slung the shotgun over his shoulder. "My dad and I got a place up here a couple o' miles over them hills. You folks can stay with us a couple of days 'til you figure out where you're gonna go and what you're gonna do."

Upon reaching the top of the hill, the view Steven, Fran, and Justin saw was awe-inspiring. You could see for miles rugged, rocky terrain, yet covered in a mixture of evergreens and grass, quite a contrast from the mountains east of Chartersville. The trail split and thinned at the top of the hill, and the man said to go left.

Steven asked the man, "So, what's your name?"

"Daniel," the man replied, "but most folks just call me Big Dan."

Steven was confused with Big Dan's answer because of the man's short stature, but he thought it best not to question it.

The trail seemed to go on forever, with Big Dan and Steven doing most of the talking. Finally, they came upon a ridge, and down below they could see a large clearing with several rustic log buildings dotting the landscape.

"That's my dad's place," Big Dan said.

All of them headed down a rock trail with switchbacks that finally led to the clearing below. When they reached the bottom, they walked across the clearing to the main cabin. Big Dan opened the door to see his dad sitting at the table with a bowl of stew in front of him and a newspaper held upward in his right hand.

Big Dan began to speak to his dad saying, "Dad, I have some people I'd like you to meet. This is Steven and his wife Fran."

Before Big Dan could say another word, his dad interrupted, "I know who they are. What are they doing here?"

"Dad, they're not what you're reading in the newspaper."

"Oh, they're not? Then you tell me who they are."

Big Dan told his dad the story that Steven had told him.

After listening intently, Big Dan's dad said, "You know, I don't think anybody could make that up. You folks can stay here, but not for long. I have no intentions of getting' mixed up in other folks' problems. You three can sleep in the old cow shed. We don't use it anymore."

Big Dan said, "Come on. I'll show you to your temporary home."

The old cow shed had four sides built from logs and a metal roof. It was a small space with a dirt floor and a hay loft above.

"This will keep you out of site. I'll bring you back some blankets before nightfall," Big Dan said as he started to leave.

Steven turned to Fran and said, "At least we're out of the weather."

Fran didn't say anything; instead, she just climbed the ladder to the loft above, lied down in the old hay, and went to sleep. Later that evening, Big Dan brought back some blankets and a big kettle of stew, along with some old tin cups and spoons. After dinner, all of them went to sleep.

The next morning, when the three woke up, the first thing out of Justin's mouth was, "I'm hungry."

Fran responded, "You're just gonna have to wait, Justin."

Just after Fran's response, Steven asked, "What's that

noise?"

"What noise?" asked Fran.

"It sounds like cars," Steven replied.

"I don't hear any cars," Justin replied in his usual loud, brash voice.

"Be quiet, Justin!" Steven said in a commanding tone.

Looking out a crack in the door, Steven could see two cars driving up the long driveway that led to the main cabin. There was a man in the car in front, probably in his mid-forties, and a younger woman driving the car behind. When both cars approached the cabin, the two got out and walked to the cabin together. The man knocked on the door.

Big Dan's dad opened it and said, "What can I do for you?"

The woman responded, "We're with the State of Wyoming Department of Criminal Investigation."

"So, what are you doing way out here?" asked Big Dan's dad.

The man responded, "We got a tip that two fugitives and a male juvenile were spotted in the area by two men hunting in the area."

"Have you seen these three?" the woman asked as she showed Big Dan's dad pictures of Steven, Fran, and Justin.

"No, I haven't seen them," replied Big Dan's dad.

The man, along with the woman, noticed a slight look of apprehension on his face and suspected he might be lying.

"Do you mind if we have a look around?" he asked.

"Actually, I do, but be my guest."

He opened the cabin door for the two, and they took a quick visual survey of the one room cabin.

Not seeing any evidence of more than two people living there, the man presented Big Dan's dad with a business card and said, "If you see these three, give us a call."

The two left, but not before taking a look in the barn that Steven could see from the cow shed. After the two left, Big Dan's dad told him to tell Steven, Fran, and Justin that the three of them had to leave.

Big Dan set down a couple of backpacks in front of them saying, "I took the liberty of packin' you folks some things you might need. Good luck!"

He then turned around and left the cow shed.

Steven looked at Fran, who by this time was rather frustrated, and Fran just said, "Let's just go."

The three of them headed up another trail from the cabin, which led further up the rocky, treed landscape.

After only about a half-hour of hiking, Fran said, "I have to rest."

Steven took this opportunity to look through the backpacks Big Dan had given them. There was a good supply of things that might come in handy: a can opener, some canned meats and crackers, trail mix, a water filtering system, a compass, hand warmers, and an assortment of other small items that would come in handy for the trip. Steven immediately made use of the compass.

At this point, Steven thought it best if they headed north. After hours of hiking over rocky terrain, spotted with trees, Steven thought he heard cars in the distance. Following the sound of traffic, the three came across a road that led northeast.

Steven knew the three couldn't continue on foot, but they would have to be very selective on how they chose to travel. It was important that they stay out of site, so high profile vehicles would be the best choice if they chose to hitchhike. This seemed like the best course of action this time, as there really wasn't any other choice at the moment. After a couple of unsuccessful attempts with tractor trailers, the three were able to secure a ride with a large recreational vehicle. As they climbed aboard, the man behind the wheel introduced himself as Stanley. He was an older man, probably in his early sixties, with a small white beard and mustache, and not much hair.

Stanley said, "Nice to have you three aboard. Where you headed?"

Steven answered, "North."

"Me too," Stanley said.

Stanley explained that he worked for a company that bought RVs directly from the manufacture and delivered them to the customers that purchased them from his company. Steven asked how someone could make such a purchase without seeing it first.

"Oh, they know what they're getting," Stanley said, "It's all virtual. They can see every detail before they make their purchase. It's very comprehensive. Been in business ten years and haven't had a complaint yet. I'm delivering this one to a retired couple just over the border, in Canada."

Steven and Fran looked at each other just after he said that, and the two of them knew what each other was thinking.

"So where are you from?" asked Stanley.

"Chartersville," answered Steven.

"Chartersville? You sure are a long way from home. How did you end up in north-central Wyoming?" Stanley asked inquisitively.

"It's a long story," Steven said once again.

"You just said 'North', and I'm headed to Canada. I've got time."

Once again, Steven told the whole story over: the police escort, their escape from the underground facility, their experiences in Vincent, the train ride, and the rest of their experiences. After intently listening to Steven's story for quite some time, there was an awkward silence that couldn't have been more than a few seconds, but for Steven and Fran, it seemed like an eternity.

After the pause, Stanley said, "You know what, I believe you. Best thing for you three to do would be to come with me to Canada."

The four of them crossed the Wyoming border into Montana, got on the interstate going north, and headed towards the first major city in Montana. After some discussion, Stanley, Steven, and Fran decided it would be best to continue heading north to the next interstate and head east before picking up their northern route in eastern Montana. It seemed as though there would be a lot less worry if they did not go into the city, but that feeling did not last long. Just on the outskirts of the small town of Hardtown, where the four needed to go to continue north to the next interstate, they could see flashers on both sides of the interstate, and there didn't appear to be any accident.

Stanley said, "You three better get out of sight."

Steven said, "Where?"

"Use the bathroom and the closet. Don't you worry, I'll talk our way out of this."

Steven told Justin to get in the closet, but Justin couldn't figure out how to open the door. Steven opened it for him, and told him to get inside and not to make a sound.

Meanwhile, Steven and Fran somehow managed to fit in the bathroom. As Stanley got closer to the flashers, he could clearly see that this was a roadblock that had been set up to screen passing vehicles. Things were very slow going. Stanley watched as the officers looked inside and talked to the drivers of the two passenger cars ahead of them.

As Stanley pulled up next to the officer, the officer said, "Good evening, sir. May I please see your license, registration, and proof of financial responsibility?"

Stanley gave the officer his license and the necessary paperwork his company had provided him.

The officer said, "According to your paperwork, you are delivering this vehicle to Canada. Is that correct?"

"Yes, sir," Stanley said, "nothing unusual for our company."

"Is the side door open?"

"Yes, it is."

The officer stepped to the side of the vehicle and opened the side door.

Just as the officer climbed up the step into the RV, another officer stepped up next to him and said, "Joe, we got a call that said three subjects fitting the description of the suspects we're looking for were seen south of here on the reservation. Sarge says we're to meet the reservation police for a search of the area. We're closing the road block up right now."

Both officers stepped down, returned to their patrol cars, and got off the interstate.

Stanley continued up the interstate as he yelled, "You three can come out now."

Steven said, "It was a little cramped in there."

Fran replied, "You're not kidding."

Stanley said, "I really thought this was the end of the road for you. You three must be the luckiest sons of bitches in the entire world."

After a few minutes of light conversation, Steven thought he heard a voice and asked Fran if she heard anything.

Fran replied, "Oh my gosh! Justin," as she got up and opened the closet door to let him out.

"What am I? Chopped liver?" asked Justin as he exited the closet. Everyone, except Justin, had a quick laugh over the incident.

Stanley turned off the interstate and headed north, to the next interstate. After traveling for about forty-five minutes, the four of them turned east. They chatted about everything for the next hour, then Stanley said he was hungry and was going to stop in the city to get something to eat. When he stopped, Steven and Fran took the opportunity to break out some of the crackers and canned meat Big Dan had given them. As they were eating, the side door opened, and a big smile appeared on Justin's face. As Steven and Fran turned to look toward the door, they could see that Stanley had returned with a tray of four drinks and a huge fast food bag.

Justin exclaimed, "Food!!"

Stanley calmly said, "I figured you three would be hungry. It's on me."

Steven and Fran thanked Stanley profusely as the food was set in front of them.

"You're welcome," replied Stanley, adding, "Just be careful. This RV has to be in tip-top condition when I deliver it to the new owners."

After a very satisfying meal, the three were rather

sleepy.

As Stanley got back onto the interstate, he said, "You know, that dining table converts into a bed if Justin wants to take a nap. You two are welcome to use the bed in the back."

Steven set the bed up for Justin, and Steven and Fran took advantage of the opportunity to get some rest.

Chapter 14

When Steven woke up, he looked out the window and saw what appeared to be a rather barren landscape.

He nudged Fran, and Fran asked, "Where are we?"

Steven replied, "I'm not sure. Let's find out."

The two of them got up, went to the front of the RV, and sat on the couch opposite Justin, who was still sound asleep.

"So, where are we?" Steven asked Stanley.

Stanley replied, "I'd say we're about two hours south of the Canadian border, somewhere on the Fort Handlan Indian reservation."

The three continued to talk about small things. Justin woke up, and Steven converted his bed back to a dining table. Stanley said he needed to stop in the small town of Cherish City. He pulled into a gas station to fill up the RV with gas. Stanley explained that it was customary for his company to do this, something that gave his company and edge over the competition. Stanley bought a soda for each of them. The four headed north toward the border.

About two miles out, Stanley said, "We're coming up on the border. You three better get your passports out."

Completely forgetting that passports would be a necessity, Steven replied, "What passports?"

"You've gotta be kidding. You three don't have passports?" Stanley continued, "Look, you three are nice people, and I feel bad for all you three have been through, but this is U.S. Customs, and I'm not risking this one. Best thing is for me to drop you three off here, and I'm afraid you're on your own."

Stanley pulled the RV to the side of the road. Steven and Fran picked up the backpacks Big Dan had given them and stepped down and opened the RV door.

Stanley said, "Good luck to you three. Hope everything turns out well for you."

After Steven, Fran, and Justin had stepped down to the side of the road, Steven shut the door behind him and the RV pulled away to continue north.

Fran looked at Steven with a frustrated face and said, "Now what?" in a tone that matched that frustration.

Steven replied calmly, "We walk."

The three then headed north on foot, but slightly to the west and away from the road to avoid being seen, not that there were any people or traffic to see them. The compass Big Dan had given them came in very handy. They walked north for what seemed like an eternity. They were getting cold, and it was starting to get dark. As night fell, the temperature dropped even more. Not knowing where they were, the three stopped to get some rest. They huddled together to keep warm. Fran leaned her head against Steven's back and started crying.

Steven thought he heard something rustling in the distance. Before he knew it, he looked up and saw a flashlight shining in his eyes. The illumination of it revealed the man holding it was wearing a bright red jacket, with a sash across it, and a brimmed hat.

With the flashlight in his left hand, it was easy to see the revolver in his right as he exclaimed loudly, "CBSA. Don't move." The CBSA agent continued to speak in a firm, but calm tone, "Steven, lie flat on your stomach, spread your arms above your head, and do not move."

When Steven had complied, the CBSA agent approached Steven, pulled his arms back, and handcuffed him.

While Steven was still lying on his stomach, the CBSA agent continued, "Fran, lie on your stomach. Place your arms above your head, spreading them apart."

Before approaching Fran, the CBSA agent looked at Justin and said, "Justin, don't try anything stupid."

The agent walked over to Fran, as Justin watched in disbelief. He pulled Fran's arms back behind her and handcuffed her with a second set of cuffs.

Training his flashlight on Justin, he said, "Justin, you too. Lie down on your stomach and put your hands above your head."

Justin complied, but the CBSA agent had to tell him to spread his arms. Justin moved his arms down in what was more of a T-position than spreading them above his head.

The CBSA agent approached Justin and said, "Sorry, Justin, I only have ties left," as he pulled Justin's arms behind him and tied them together at the wrists. "This is more for my safety than anything else," he said as he continued with his instructions. "Justin, pull your knees up when I say."

"Now," said the CBSA agent, and with some struggle, he managed to get Justin on his feet.

He repeated the procedure for both Steven and Fran and told the three of them to walk directly in front of him and to follow his instructions on where to walk. After a very short walk in the cold, dark night, the four of them approached a larger vehicle, obviously four-wheel drive, with a light bar on top.

The CBSA agent opened the back door for Steven first and said, "Watch your head," as he pushed slightly down on Steven's head, and Steven got in the back. The agent did the same for Justin, and then Fran, last.

As the CBSA agent got behind the wheel, shut the door, and started the car, Justin asked, "How do you know our names?"

The CBSA agent replied, "Every law enforcement agency in North America knows your names."

"So where do we go from here?" asked Steven.

"We're taking you to Elkmont, where you'll be processed and later transported to the larger city of Reibers."

"Are they going to send us back to the U.S?"

"That is for a Canadian court to decide."

"We didn't even know we were in Canada," Fran said.

"Based on what I know, you're probably better off being in Canada at this point," replied the CBSA agent.

The ride fell silent the remainder of the trip. Upon arriving at the patrol station in Elkmont, the CBSA agent pulled behind the building, through a small parking lot, and up next to a metal double door. After getting out, he opened the back door of the patrol vehicle and got the three of them out. He slid a card through a reader mounted on the wall next to the door and pulled the door open.

Inside, there was a well-lit room with a white tile floor and walls painted white. In front of them were metal detectors and two border agents next to them, one male and one female. The male agent patted Steven and Justin down, while the female agent patted Fran down. Upon going through the metal detectors, there were four metal desks and chairs, two on each side of the room. In the back of the room, there was an office with a reinforced glass wall overlooking the room.

A tall, thin, gentleman, probably in is mid-thirties and wearing a suit, poked his head out the door and said, "Casey, bring those three in here."

Casey walked the three over to the office, and upon entering, Steven could see that there was a series of seats on the left against the wall and a desk on the right in the center of the office.

The tall man said, "Steven, Fran, Justin. Sit down," motioning to the seats against the wall.

Once the three were seated, the man introduced himself as Jeff Monarch, director the CBSA, "I am responsible for the area where you three crossed the border. The U.S. Government has filled us in on your fugitive status. Based on the instructions I have received from my supervisors, we're going to put you three together in a separate holding cell overnight, until we can take you to Reibers in the morning.

"We're not fugitives," replied Steven. "Listen, you've gotta help us."

Jeff interrupted, "All three of you will have an opportunity to plead your case before a provincial judge in

Reibers." At that, he pushed a button on the phone and said, "Send Casey back in here."

When Casey came into the office, Jeff said, "Take these three to holding cell three."

"You want all three in the same holding cell, Jeff?"

"Just do it, Casey," Jeff replied.

Casey took the three to the holding cell, opened the door, released the three from their handcuffs, and locked the door to the cell. It was a large cell with two beds on each side, one directly above the other. Justin asked where the bathroom was, and Fran pointed to a stainless steel fixture against the wall that combined the sink and the toilet.

"How do you close the door?" asked Justin.

"You don't," replied Fran.

"But I gotta go!"

"Then go."

"I can't go there!" Justin replied in a frustrated voice.

"Then I guess you're not going to go, are you?"

"Don't watch!!" Justin said as he headed for the toilet. Shortly after that, the three lied down and went to sleep.

Chapter 15

Morning came, and Steven woke up just before Fran. As he got down off the bed above Fran, the noise woke Fran up.

Steven jokingly asked, "What's for breakfast, sweetheart?"

"Don't you sweetheart me," replied Fran.

Just as Steven said that, a guard rolled a cart up to the outside of their cell. The guard handed each of them a foil tray with plastic wrap labeled "French Toast with Eggs Breakfast". The breakfasts were barely warm. The only drink offered was water, but Steven, Fran, and Justin were still happy to get this.

Shortly after the three ate, a CBSA officer approached the cell and said, "I've been instructed to take you three to Reibers."

He opened the cell door, and put handcuffs back on all three of them. He led them out of the building to a waiting patrol vehicle. Once the three were in the patrol vehicle, the officer headed east toward Reibers.

"I'm not sure I understand the Canadian justice system. Can you tell me what's going to happen?" Steven asked the officer.

The officer replied, "You'll have an opportunity to plead your case before a provincial judge. If he feels you three should be extradited, he will grant an approval to proceed. You'll be sent to another court for an extradition hearing, where a decision will be made on whether to release you to U.S. authorities."

Upon arriving in Reibers, the officer once again pulled

the patrol vehicle to the back of the building, where there were two metal doors. The officer got Steven, Fran, and Justin out of the patrol vehicle, slid a card through the card reader mounted next to the door, opened the door, and told Steven, Fran, and Justin to step through.

Once inside, once again, there was a large well-lit room with a white tile floor. Again, there were desks in the room, although significantly more this time.

The CBSA officer led the three through the room, then made a right down a hallway that had a series of doors on the right. At the third door, the CBSA officer once again slid his card through a reader mounted on the right of the door. This time, before opening the door, he waited for a buzzer to sound.

Inside, on the right, there were four chairs against the wall, and on the left, there was a desk in the center of the room. The man behind it was standing in front of his chair. He was a tall, thin man, in his middle to late fifties with a short haircut and graying hair. He wore a well-tailored blue suit, dress shirt, and tie. There was a CBSA pin and three gold emblems just below worn on the lapel of his suit. He gave a nod to the CBSA officer, who released the cuffs on all three and left the room. The man behind the desk broke his silence and said each of their names while making eye contact with each of them.

He then said, "You three can sit down." He continued, "I'm Brian Anderson, vice president of enforcement for the CBSA. The Canadian Government is aware of some inconsistencies in the U.S. Government account of the alleged crimes you three have committed in the U.S. As a result, in an unusual move for the CBSA, an ongoing investigation has already been launched by the CBSA concerning your case. Based on the preliminary results of this investigation, I've been asked to set up a meeting with you three and Canada's Minister of Public Safety Do you have any idea who the Minister of Public Safety is?" Mr. Anderson asked in an astonished voice, as though very few Canadians would ever meet this man.

"No, who is he?" Steven asked.

"Canada's Minister of Public Safety is responsible for

virtually every law enforcement agency in Canada, including this one."

"What's next?"

"There is an awaiting motorcade outside. You three will be taken to the airport to board a government jet and fly to Ottawa. That's all I can tell you at this stage in the game."

Brian pushed a button on his phone as he picked up the handset and said, "Send Dave in here."

He pushed a button, and the door buzzed. Another CBSA officer came inside.

Mr. Anderson looked at Dave, and said, "It's a go."

Dave led the three further down the hallway to the last door on the right. The four of them descended a metal staircase, and at the bottom, there was a door that opened into a dark parking garage with only minimal lighting. There were only CBSA vehicles. They walked into an elevator that took them to another level. There were no vehicles parked on this level, with the exception of the awaiting motorcade. The motorcade consisted of two police bikes, a black SUV, two limousines, and a patrol car in the back.

Dave opened the back door to the second limousine and said, "Get in, and good luck."

Steven wasn't exactly sure what the CBSA officer meant with that statement; nonetheless, he followed the officer's instructions. The motorcade proceeded toward a garage door that opened as the motorcycles approached it. As the garage door opened, the motorcade turned right and made its way to the airport. Upon arriving at the airport, an airport worker in an orange vest opened a chain link gate, and the motorcade proceeded directly onto the tarmac. The motorcade continued to a small white jet with two red stripes and a Canadian Government symbol just under the front window on the nose. After sitting next to the jet for a few minutes, a man in a suit opened the door to the limousine on the side next to the plane and told the three of them to slide out. As they got out, there was another man in a suit who followed them as the first one led them up the stairs. Inside the plane, there were four wide vinyl seats that faced each other. Directly behind them, there were two more identical seats with a table between them. Directly across from the table was a vinyl couch.

The three of them were asked to take a seat in the front of the plane and to fasten their seat belts. The door was closed, and soon after, the plane taxied from the tarmac to the runway. The plane stopped for a minute and Steven, Fran, and Justin could hear the loud rev of the jet engines powering up. It wasn't long after that the jet began a very fast ascent using the runway and was in the air.

There was some silence at the beginning of the flight, but it was broken when Justin asked, "Dad, where are we going?"

Steven answered Justin, "To see a man I think is going to help us."

The seats on the plane were very comfortable and all three used this opportunity to get some sleep on the two and half-hour flight to Ottawa. It wasn't long until the plane began its descent. After landing in Ottawa, the jet taxied over to the tarmac where, once again, there was another waiting motorcade. After boarding the limousine, the motorcade proceeded through the streets of Ottawa, arriving at the capitol building a short time thereafter. The motorcade proceeded to a secure entrance.

Once inside, the three were escorted down a long hallway. At the end of the hallway, they were required to pass through metal detectors. Once through, the three of them and their escorts proceeded further down the hallway, which seemed to "T" at the end. One of the men with them slid a card through the reader and punched a code into the keypad. There were now doors to offices on both sides of the hallway. At the end of this hallway stood two armed security guards and another set of doors. One of the men that was with the three showed one of the guards at the door a pink sheet of paper. The guard radioed a message in what must have been code, and shortly thereafter, the door buzzed. Inside was a beautiful lobby tastefully decorated in French decor.

The three continued through the lobby and met with a tall, distinguished-looking gentleman, dressed in what Steven thought to be one of the most expensive suits he ever saw in his life.

The man introduced himself, saying, "Good evening. I'm Jason Culver, Canada's Minister of Public Safety. I understand you three have had an opportunity to experience some unexpected turn of events in your life. Would you say that's a fair statement?" Jason asked in a rather calm voice.

Steven answered, "That would be the understatement of the year," in response.

"Why don't we go to my office, where we can talk about this in further detail?"

He led the three of them a little further through the lobby, to a wooden door designed to match the French decor. Once inside, the three could see that the office was also decorated in French decor, although it had a slight masculine tone to it. The walls were painted in a light brown, accented by white trim throughout. It was a large office with leather furniture. In the center of the office were two chairs facing a couch with a large oval coffee table between them. Jason asked the three of them to sit down. Steven and Fran took a seat on the couch, while Jason and Justin took a seat in each of the chairs.

Jason began to speak, "I am well aware of your experiences. You are here because I personally wanted to have an opportunity to hear your version of them. I pride myself on ensuring that Canada's justice system is fair and impartial. Hearing your version of the events that have transpired will allow me to do just that, as I have full confidence in the investigations of the law enforcement agencies this office oversees."

Steven once again relayed all the events that took place since they were first stopped in Chartersville, sparing no detail, and as always, feeling slightly relieved getting their story out, in the hopes that this time the person they were talking to would have the autonomy to put their lives back into some sort of order. After a lengthy conversation, Jason revealed that the three of them would be guests of the Canadian Government.

Not sure of what Jason meant, Steven asked, "So where do we go from here?"

Jason replied, "You will be escorted to your stateroom. Unfortunately, we cannot allow you access to public media; however, we have an extensive library of videos for your enjoyment."

Justin blurted out, "What about video games and books?"

Jason answered, "You'll find an extensive library of books in your stateroom. As for the video games, I'll see what I can do."

Looking once again at Steven, Jason said, "Steven, inside your stateroom, you'll find a menu containing guest of state services. Please make use of it."

The three were escorted to their accommodations. The door to the stateroom was opened for them, and inside was a large suite, with the living area decorated in beautiful French decor. The walls were painted a light blue, and accented with white trim. The room was tastefully decorated in French Victorian furniture that was carefully chosen to give the room an appearance of grandeur. The bedroom was equally tasteful, maintaining the suites French Victorian decor. The bathroom contained a large, claw-foot tub with gold feet and trim to match. There were two pedestal sinks and a large Victorian-style mirror above them. Next to the toilet was another porcelain fixture, obviously a bidet.

It took no time for Justin to ask, "What is that for?"

Fran smiled at Justin and said, "It's used for cleaning your butt."

"How?"

"I'll let you figure that out."

In the living area next to the phone, there was a covered menu with a black cover embossed in gold lettering that read "Complementary Guest of State Services". Inside there were four groupings. The first contained a cover page that simply read "State Menu". It was followed by a listing of entrees, beverages, and desserts that would satisfy the pallet of any guest of state. The next grouping contained a list of concierge services. This was followed by a third cover page that read "Wardrobe". This section contained four headings: "Men's Store", "Lady's Wear", "Young Men's", and "Young Lady's". These subgroups contained an array of clothing that would be acceptable for any guest of state. The last cover page simply stated "Additional Services" and was followed by a list of services that might be utilized by government officials from other countries.

Steven told Fran, "You gotta see this," referring to the menu.

Just then, Justin's voice could be heard coming from the bathroom, yelling, "Oh, now I know what it's for!"

As Fran walked into the bathroom, she could see the wet floor.

She looked at Justin and said, "Your going to clean that up!" in a stern voice.

Steven decided to take a bath while Fran ordered clothing and food for all three of them. The clothing arrived while Steven was still taking a bath. On the cart below was a Funzone 3, still in the box with an assortment of ten of the newest games accompanying it. Fran took Steven the fine dress pants and shirt provided.

Steven asked, "Didn't they have jeans and a T-shirt?"

Fran replied, "No, they don't. Just wear what they gave us."

When Steven came out, Fran took a bath. Meanwhile, the food Fran ordered arrived. Steven and Justin ate while Fran was in the bath. Fran yelled from the bathroom for Steven to bring her the clothes that were delivered for her. She came out of the bathroom wearing an expensive looking pair of charcoal gray slacks and a white blouse that complimented the slacks to nothing less than perfection.

She looked at Steven and asked, "How do I look?"

Steven replied, "Beautiful," in the tone of voice that

assured Fran this was a very honest answer.

Fran just smiled for a second and then looked at Justin and said, "It's your turn."

"Turn for what?" Justin asked.

"To take a bath," Fran replied in a voice that implied the answer was obvious.

Justin reluctantly headed for the bathroom and took a bath. After Justin had his bath, he made good use of the video game that was sent up. After Justin went to bed, Fran chose a movie from those provided. Steven took the opportunity to get some much needed sleep. In the morning, Fran ordered breakfast off the guest of state menu. A short time later, breakfast was delivered to the stateroom. After breakfast, the phone rang. Steven answered, and on the other end was Jason again.

Jason asked, "I trust your overnight accommodations were suitable."

"More than suitable," replied Steven.

"I'm glad to hear that," replied Jason. There was a short pause and Jason continued, "Steven, based on the results of our preliminary investigation, the Canadian Government feels it would be in your best interest if you three were provided with a more suitable location. I'm sending an escort to your room. You won't need to take anything with you. The Canadian Government will provide what you need."

A short time later, the escort arrived in his room. The three of them were taken through a series of hallways that eventually led to an exit. Once outside, there was an awaiting helicopter.

Fran asked Steven, "Is that for us?"

Steven replied, "Do you see anybody else here?"

The three boarded the helicopter. Once on board, the pilot handed each of them a headset and said, "Here, put these on. It's gonna get noisy in here."

All three fastened their harnesses and the pilot checked them and then fired up the engine. The rotors began to spin at the speed necessary for take-off, and shortly thereafter, the helicopter was airborne. The scenery from the air was beautiful.

Steven asked, "Can you tell us where we're going?"

"To a secure location."

Not knowing exactly what that meant and seeing a look of apprehension on Fran's face, Steven said, "Everything is going to be OK, Fran."

The flight took about an hour and forty-five minutes, and the helicopter set down in a clearing in the woods. Waiting for them was an older, heavier man, probably in his mid-fifties. He wore blue jeans, a checkered flannel shirt, and a brown cowboy hat, which he held on his head firmly as the helicopter landed.

On the ground, rotors still spinning, the pilot looked at the three of them and said, "This man is going to take you to your temporary home."

After the three exited the helicopter, the pilot took off, and the man with them said, "I've been instructed to take you to a secure location."

Steven answered and said, "I'm Steven. This is my wife Fran, and son, Justin."

The man replied, "No you're not. Someone else will let you know who you are. For now, just follow me."

The man led them to a newer, four-door sedan parked on a gravel driveway next to the roadway. Steven got in the passenger's seat, while Fran and Justin got in the back. The man drove them to a two-story, cedar-sided cabin just outside of town. When they arrived, they were met by another man at the car. He opened the door, and the three slid out.

The man looked at the three and said, "Introductions later. Let's get you inside."

Once inside the cabin, the man introduced himself as Jeff Laskin, with the CNFIS. He explained that although this was an unusual assignment for him, he has been instructed to provide protective services for Steven, Fran, and Justin.

The cabin itself was beautiful. It was very open on the first floor, and it was furnished with log furniture to match the knotted wood siding on the walls. There was a large, stone fireplace against the wall in the living area. Although Steven and Fran knew this would be their temporary home, strangely, they felt comfortable here. The refrigerator and cupboards were well stocked. Upstairs were closets full of clothing that was selected to fit each of them. The cabin was equipped with everything they would need.

Jeff instructed Steven, Fran, and Justin not to answer the door.

Steven asked Jeff, "Who is going to be looking for us here?"

Jeff answered, "When it comes to national investigations, borders don't mean a lot. It's my job to keep you out of sight until our government has an opportunity to complete its investigation."

Jeff continued, "A few simple rules. Like I said before, don't answer the door. Keep away from the windows. You are not to leave the cabin for any reason. If you need something, you go through me. Understood?" asked Jeff.

Steven replied, "You're the boss," in a voice that indicated that Steven felt as though he no longer had the power to make his own decisions, something he felt very uncomfortable with.

Justin asked, "Where do I sleep?"

Fran took Justin upstairs to the smaller bedroom, where he promptly laid down on the bed to get what he felt was some much needed rest, although it was only mid-afternoon.

When Fran came back downstairs, she asked Steven if he wanted to watch TV.

"What TV?" replied Steven.

Fran walked over to a knotted pine cabinet against the wall in the living area and promptly opened the doors to reveal a thirty-six inch HD color TV and a VCR with a library of videos on the shelves below it. It seemed Fran had a knack for finding the TV, wherever it might be.

Thinking of Steven this time, Fran pulled out a romantic comedy from the shelves below the TV and looked at

Steven with movie in hand and said, "Do you want to watch this?"

"I guess so," Steven replied.

Years of marriage had given Fran the ability to know when Steven needed to unwind, and this was on of those times. The two watched the movie together, and the movie did seem to provide a temporary sense of relief from the stress created by all the events that had taken place up to this point. After the movie, Fran decided to prepare a lunch for the four of them.

A few hours later, there was a knock at the door. Jeff told Steven, Fran, and Justin to stay where they were, then he proceeded to answer the door. He cautiously opened the door and discovered it was his partner who had been sent to relieve him. Jeff introduced his partner to Steven and Fran as David Bryar. Jeff explained that the two of them would be taking twelve-hour shifts.

Several days went by, and Steven and Fran received word through Jeff that the Canadian Government had concluded its investigation of their case. As a result, the Canadian Government would be working actively with the U.S. Government to reach an agreement that would be amicable to everyone involved. In the interim, the CNFIS felt it would be in Steven, Fran, and Justin's best interest if they were to stay right where they were at this point.

Steven asked Jeff, "So what exactly does this mean for us?"

Jeff replied, "Steven, basically, I am liaison for the CNFIS. I do what I'm assigned to do, and I do it well. If you're asking me to interpret what I've been told to tell you, it would be nothing more than my personal opinion."

"That would be good enough for me."

"Based on my years of experience in this field, it would be my belief that you're going to come out on the winning side of this thing."

Steven, Fran, and Justin resigned themselves to the fact that they may be there for a while, but they took heart in the fact that Jeff believed that the Canadian Government would be working in Steven, Fran, and Justin's best interest. The cabin was comfortable, and looking back at their past experiences, they certainly were right where they needed to be for the moment.

As the days passed, Fran became rather comfortable with her surroundings, and she tried to make a home for her family, even if it did include a private security detail twenty-four hours a day. Fran couldn't help but think about her oldest son Joshua, who lived with her mother and father in the northwest part of the state in New Mexico. She certainly wondered how he was doing, and if he knew about all the experiences she, Steven, and Justin had been through.

Chapter 16

Meanwhile, in Chartersville, peace had been restored, though, not before much devastation had undertaken the city at the hands of its own citizens. Buildings had been burned. Cars had been overturned, and businesses were looted in the midst of the chaos. Once order had been restored in the city, martial law was imposed, and ironically, the people in Chartersville found themselves in the same situation they had been previously, confined to their homes indoors. John Clemens had been removed from his position as the city's Bio-Hazard Safety Director and the "National Institute of Health" had taken over the office.

Due to the recent events that had taken place in Chartersville, the NIH was working with the Department of Justice to determine what agencies would prosecute the crimes that had taken place in the city from the onset of the alleged bio-hazard threat. At the top of their list was the disclosure of information that could pose a risk to national security, and that is the reason the Department of Justice would be handling all negotiations with the Canadian Government concerning decisions being made in matters concerning Steven, Fran, and Justin. Both the U.S. and Canadian Government were well aware that the negotiations concerning the three of them would be a rather long process, as the Canadian Government had made it clear to the U.S. Government, through conversations with Canada's Minister of Public Safety and the U.S. Attorney General, that Canada had full intentions of making absolutely sure that whatever the results of the negotiations were, they would be in the best interest of Steven, Fran, and Justin.

***

Meanwhile, in the small town of Drilton, in the northwest part of New Mexico, Fran's mother was constantly on the phone with every law enforcement and state agency in the state trying to find Steven, Fran, and Justin. Even with her persistent calls, it seemed she was having no luck whatsoever.

Frustrated with the lack of progress his grandmother was making in trying to find his family, Joshua decided to take it upon himself to find his parents and brother. Remembering the newscast he saw on TV that stated his parents had escaped from prison and knowing this not to be true, Joshua thought it best to start looking in Vincent, where the newscast had stated his parents were last seen. So Joshua bought a one-way ticket from Drilton to Vincent, although Fran's mother thought this trip was a bad idea. After all, Joshua was twenty years old now and was able to make his own decisions, so she agreed to take him to the bus station. He made sure to talk to his boss and explain the need for the time off, and because of his stellar attendance record in the past, and knowing that he was a good employee, his boss agreed to give him two weeks off.

Joshua wasn't shy about asking people for help, so when the bus arrived at the station in Vincent, he asked the man behind the counter at the bus station if he knew of the convenience store where two alleged prison escapees supposedly stole a car and took off.

The man behind they counter responded, "Everyone in Vincent knows about that. Not too much like that happens around here."

"How do I get there?" Joshua asked.

The man responded, "Three blocks north of here on your right."

Joshua figured he could walk three blocks, so he started on foot toward the convenience store. He passed one convenience store, but knew the man at the bus station said three blocks. Joshua was meticulous about following directions, so he continued up the street to the next convenience store and asked the woman behind the counter if she knew anything about the alleged stolen car incident.

"Alleged?!" the woman responded emphatically, "I was there when it happened! Nothing alleged about it."

Not wanting to believe his parents would commit such a crime, Joshua just asked if she knew where they went.

The woman responded, "If I knew where they went, I would have already told the police. That poor guy was one of my regular customers. You know, you sort of look like the man. I didn't get a good look at him when he stole the car, but I saw both of their pictures on the news. Who is he to you? Or both of them for that matter?"

Joshua just said, "Thanks," and walked out of the convenience store.

As he left, the woman he was talking to ran out the door after him and said, "Look, kid. The last I heard, the state police found my customer's car just north of town in Fort Brazen, Colorado. He got it back yesterday. Nothing wrong with it. The cops were keeping the darn thing all this time for evidence."

"Where's Fort Brazen?" Joshua asked.

The woman answered, "Wait here." She went back inside, came out, and handed Joshua a map of Colorado.

Joshua said, "Thanks," and when the woman went back inside, he opened the map up, found Fort Brazen, and promptly folded it into a usable position, anticipating formulating a plan to get there.

Looking at the map, Joshua saw that Fort Brazen was along a U.S. highway, so he headed back to the bus station in hopes of buying a ticket there. When he arrived, the man that he had talked to was locking the building up, and Joshua asked about a ticket to Fort Brazen.

The man responded, "Well, Fort Brazen is on one of our routes, but we don't normally stop there. I suppose I could get the driver to make an exception and stop there. No station there, though." The man continued, "You know, that bus comes through here in a couple of hours. I was going to go to lunch and come back, but I suppose I could just order a pizza. Come back inside, and I'll sell you a ticket."

Joshua bought a ticket that the man had pro-rated to cover only the distance from Vincent to Fort Brazen. He spent the time waiting for the bus on the computer. He always had his laptop with him. It wasn't long before a car pulled up and delivered the man behind the counter his pizza. Joshua just tried to bury himself deeper into his work, as the pizza smelled really good and he was hungry.

After about twenty minutes, the man behind the counter yelled, "Hey kid, you want the rest of this? I can't eat it all."

Joshua said, "Yes."

He thanked the man and ate the two slices that were left. Working on the computer was one of Joshua's favorite activities, and the time waiting for the bus seemed to fly by. When he boarded, there were only a few people on it, and Joshua took a seat next to the window. He spent the three hour ride to Fort Brazen continuing to work on his computer, only taking a brief moment to look out the window when he felt the need. Once again, the time seemed to pass by quickly, and the bus driver pulled the bus into a small parking lot in front of a small convenience store with two gas pumps.

The driver opened the door and said, "Fort Brazen."

As Joshua looked out the window, all he saw was the convenience store and a couple of houses. Joshua asked the driver in his usual manner, believing he already knew the answer, "Are you sure this is Fort Brazen?"

The driver responded, "Look kid, I've been doing this for over thirty years. This is Fort Brazen!"

Joshua apprehensively got off the bus and walked toward the convenience store as the bus pulled away behind him. As he went to pull open the door, he discovered it was locked. It was getting to be dusk, and fear was the first emotion that entered Joshua's mind. He sat on the steps of the convenience store contemplating what he was going to do next. Shortly thereafter, a small, late-model, silver two-door Coupe pulled up next to the pumps. A girl in her mid-twenties, wearing red jogging pants and a gray hooded sweatshirt, got out of the car. She walked over to the pumps and inserted her credit card, punched in her debit number, and began to fill her tank. Feeling he was out of options, Joshua walked over to her and asked her where the police station was.

The girl responded with, "What police station?" with an emphasis on the word "what" that could only mean there was no police station.

"What do you need a police station for, anyway?" the girl asked.

"Never mind," Joshua responded.

Sensing no threat from Joshua, and wanting to help, the girl looked at him and said, "Look, there's a state police outpost west of here in Sand City. I'll take you there if you like."

Joshua responded, "I really need to find the Fort Brazen police department."

"Look, I just told you there is no police department here. I can tell you're not from here. It's getting dark, and there's nothing here. Let me take you to Sand City."

Knowing that he was out of options at the moment, and computing in his mind that riding into the city with the girl was probably the only choice he had at this moment, Joshua agreed to take the ride. The girl hung the nozzle back on the pump, got back in the car, and unlocked the passenger door for Joshua. He opened the door and sat down in the passenger's seat, still apprehensive about taking the ride. The girl reached her hand over in an attempt to introduce herself. He just looked at her hand with an expression of confusion on his face, and then looked away.

As the girl pulled her hand back, she said, "My name is Jordan. What's yours?"

Joshua responded with nothing more than the word, "Josh."

After an awkward pause, Jordan said, "You don't talk much, do you?" With no response from Joshua, she continued, "So, you never told me why you were going to see the cops," phrasing her statement in more of a question than a statement.

Joshua responded, "I'm looking for my parents."

"What has that got to do with the cops in Sand City?"

"Fort Brazen is the last place I heard my parents were at."

"What were your parents doing in Fort Brazen?"

Figuring it was already on the news, Joshua answered, "I heard the police found a car my parents were driving there."

"You don't mean the car those two escaped convicts were driving. Oh my God! Those are you're parents?!" Jordan asked in an astonished tone of voice.

"There not convicts!" Joshua responded emphatically.

There was a short pause, and then Jordan said, "Look, I don't want to get mixed up in anything. I'll drop you off in Sand City, and then you're on your own."

Joshua thought to himself that that was all he needed anyway. What he didn't know is that Jordan meant that she had no intention of dropping him off in front of the state police outpost.

Chapter 17

When the two of them arrived in Sand City, Jordan pulled the car over in the parking lot of a well-lit gas station and said, "The state police outpost is three blocks to the east."

Joshua responded, "We should be there in a couple of minutes, then."

Jordan replied, "Look, kid, don't you get it? You're on your own, now."

"You want me to walk to the state police building?"

"Yes," Jordan replied, stretching out the word to indicate the answer was obvious.

Joshua got out of the car and started toward the convenience store, which was obviously open this time.

Jordan yelled out the window, "Good luck to you. I hope you find your parents."

When Joshua went into the convenience store, there were several people in line. Ignoring the customers in line, Joshua looked at the clerk behind the counter and asked, "Where is the state police outpost?"

A customer who was in line, responding to Joshua's question, said, "You go out the door. Make a right. Go down three blocks, and it'll be on your right. It's not marked well, but there's usually a trooper's car parked in front of it."

When Joshua arrived at the outpost, there was indeed a trooper's car in front of it. Joshua went inside, and there were two uniformed officers behind a counter.

One of them said to Joshua, "Can I help you?"

This officer was a young man, probably in his mid-twenties, with a marine style haircut. He looked like he had not been on the force long. The other officer behind the counter was older, probably in his mid-forties, about 5'7", with his hair balding in the middle.

Joshua answered the first with, "I'm looking for my parents."

"Are they missing?" asked the trooper.

"Yes."

"When was the last time you heard from them?"

"It's been a little over a month, now."

The officer replied, "Your parents have been missing over a month and you're just coming to us now? What's your name, kid?"

Sensing this was not going to go well, Joshua just replied, "Josh."

"Do you have any ID?" the officer asked.

Joshua just replied, "Yes."

"Well, can I see it?" asked the officer.

Joshua reluctantly pulled his ID from his wallet and handed it to the officer.

The officer looked at the ID, and with a surprised look on his face, looked straight at Josh and asked, "You're Joshua Fruskin?"

Joshua just looked down as the officer said, "Wait here."

The two officers stepped through a door behind the counter, which led to another room.

Confident they were out of earshot, the younger officer asked the other, "Do you know who we have here?"

The older officer replied, "I know exactly who we have here. I know what you're thinking. The APB is for his parents, not for him. We can't hold him."

"What about a tail?" asked the younger officer.

"My guess is the feds are already doing that, and if they're not, then they know where Steven and Fran are, and they're not telling us for a reason. There's nothing on the computer for Joshua. Cut him loose."

The two officers returned to the other room, and the

younger one said, "Joshua, we know all about your parents."

"So where are they?"

"I'm sorry. We can't disclose that information."

"Why?"

"Because that would be interfering with a federal investigation."

"Well, what can you tell me?"

"I'm afraid I can't tell you anything. Like I said, it's a federal matter."

Joshua left the state police outpost, believing he had not made any progress at all and already contemplating what his next move would be. As he left the building so did the older officer, who proceeded to get behind the wheel of his patrol car.

He drove up next to Joshua and asked him, "Where are you staying?"

Joshua replied, "I don't know."

"There's a Motel 17 just down the road. Get in. I'll take you there."

Joshua started to open the back door behind the officer.

The officer said, "No, the other side. Get in the front."

Joshua walked to the other side of the car and got in the front seat.

The officer pulled the patrol car onto the street and said, "Look, Josh, I know how you feel. I just lost my dad last month. I could lose my job for this, but I can tell you a state agency in Wyoming was investigating an incident where two hunters allegedly spotted your parents in central Wyoming."

"What state agency?" asked Joshua.

"The Wyoming Department of Criminal Investigation. That's all I can tell you," the trooper said as he pulled into the parking lot of the motel.

Joshua told the officer, "Thank you," as he got out of the patrol car and walked toward the motel. He rented the least expensive, non-smoking room the hotel had to offer. It was on the upper level in the center part of the two-story motel. The room had one queen bed, a dresser with a TV on top of it, and a table and chairs next to the window. There was also a nightstand and a lamp on each side of the bed.

Joshua set his laptop on the table, opened it up, and looked up the Wyoming Department of Criminal Investigation. The agency had its own website. There was a link to open cases, and Joshua clicked on it. He found a list of current cases the department was working on. They were arranged by category, and one of the sub-categories was entitled, "Fugitives at Large". About three cases down under this category, Joshua saw one that read "Case 378910" in blue lettering. Right below it were the words, "Steven Fruskin, Fran Fruskin". Joshua clicked on the case number and saw a short paragraph that read, "Steven Fruskin and Fran Fruskin are wanted by the Wyoming Department of Criminal Investigation and law enforcement agencies in the states of New Mexico, Colorado, and Montana. If you have any information regarding the whereabouts of Steven Fruskin and/or Fran Fruskin, the Wyoming Department of Criminal Investigation encourages you to contact them."

The paragraph was followed by the word "Tips" in blue just below it. Joshua clicked on the word and found a list of alleged sightings that were organized from top to bottom by the most recent date. The first listed an alleged sighting of Steven and Fran traveling with a minor in a very rural area in north central Wyoming. The one right below listed a sighting by two hunters in north central Wyoming in the same area. Joshua remembered that the trooper just said central Wyoming, but a gut feeling told him this website had the correct information. Joshua thought his best option was to take a bus to Cheyenne, where the Wyoming Department of Criminal Investigation was based. He knew that the further this trip took him, the more he would deplete his college fund, but he was intent on finding his parents and brother. Content with what his plans were for tomorrow morning, Joshua decided to turn in for the night.

Chapter 18

The next morning, Joshua got up and took a few minutes to look up the location of the bus station in Sand City on his laptop. He discovered the bus station was downtown and decided to take a city bus there. According to the information on his laptop, the two were right next to each other. When Joshua checked out of the motel, he asked the desk clerk where he could catch the city bus to the bus station. She told him there was a city bus stop just up the street, and he headed for it. When the city bus arrived downtown, Joshua discovered that the two stations were indeed next to each other, practically one building, as two walkways connected the buildings together. Joshua walked to the other building and, this time, found a rather large lobby area with rows of seats and a few seats with coin operated televisions attached to them.

Joshua walked up to the counter, and there was a tall man, about six feet in height, probably in his mid-fifties, with a shiny bald head, behind the counter. He was wearing a uniform and was on the phone. After the man got off the phone, he asked Joshua if he could help him.

Joshua said, "I need to buy a ticket to Cheyenne, Wyoming."

"Round trip or one-way?" asked the man.

"One-way."

"That bus leaves at 2:10 PM today, and arrives in Cheyenne at 1:30 AM tomorrow morning."

Not knowing what he was going to do for five hours while waiting for the bus, but, having no choice, he said, "That will be fine."

Joshua asked if they had free Wi-Fi, and the man said they did. Joshua was glad he had recharged his laptop overnight at the motel. He spent the time working a new computer program he was working on, so into what he was doing the hours flew by, and he didn't even think about getting anything to eat.

The next thing Joshua knew, he heard these words over the PA system, "Bus 57 now departing from gate three with service to Pueblo, Colorado Springs, Denver, Boulder, Fort Collins, and Cheyenne, Wyoming. All ticketed passengers please board at gate three now."

Feeling his hunger now, Joshua took a chance and grabbed something from the vending machines before boarding the bus. When he boarded, there were only aisle seats available. Most of the passengers did not appear to be the kind of people Joshua was used to seeing, and he continued walking toward the back of the bus. On his right, toward the back, there was a girl about his age with an empty seat next to her.

This was the only open window seat on the whole bus, and Joshua asked, "Is that seat taken?"

The girl replied, "No, not at all," and got up to let Joshua in.

Joshua sat down and looked out the window as the girl next to him continued to read the book she was reading. The bus pulled out of the station, continued through town, and then headed east on the same U.S. Route Joshua was on previously. Time passed, and the bus finally reached the interstate. The bus turned north onto the interstate and continued its journey.

Shortly thereafter, the girl sitting next to Joshua put down her book, turned toward him, and said, "So, we haven't been properly introduced. I'm Jennie O'Share. And you are?"

"Joshua Fruskin," replied Joshua.

"Fruskin. Where have I heard that name before?" Jennie replied, meaning to ask herself the question.

Joshua didn't respond, and more interested in having a conversation than continuing with the awkward silence that had prevailed since the bus left the station, Jennie continued with her inquisitions, "Where are you headed?"

"Cheyenne."

"Cheyenne, Wyoming? So what's in Cheyenne, anyway?"

"Some information I need," Joshua replied in the same mundane manner.

"Boy, you're a real fountain of information, aren't you?" Jennie asked Joshua sarcastically.

"I answered your questions, didn't I?"

"Didn't your parents teach you anything about how to treat a girl?"

"Excuse me?" Joshua asked, wanting to know what she was talking about.

Jennie continued, "Look, I'm not getting off until Fort Collins, and you're going to Cheyenne, so that means we have to spend the next several hours sitting next to each other, and I'd like to make this trip a pleasant one."

Joshua just looked at her with a look that appeared to say, "What the hell is she talking about?" Joshua continued to work on his laptop, thinking that the conversation he had just reinforced his belief that girls were a breed of their own.

The bus continued north, and the awkward silence continued while Jennie read her book and Joshua continued to work on his computer, although Joshua didn't think the silence was uncomfortable at all. He just looked at it as an opportunity to get more done. Slightly upset, Jennie decided to change seats, but by this time, the bus had stopped in a couple of small towns and picked up more passengers, and now there were no other seats available. So for the time being, Jennie just sank into her book to pass the time.

It wasn't too long after that when the bus driver made an announcement over the loudspeaker, "Folks, we will be stopping for a thirty minute delay in Rikersville. You will have an opportunity to purchase a late lunch and some snacks here. Please be back on the bus five minutes prior to departure."

Moments later, the bus exited the interstate and made a right turn. Just down the street, the bus pulled into what appeared to be a fast-food/chain-convenience store combination. Joshua was rather hungry now, and he opted for a bacon cheeseburger meal over snacks from the convenience store. He got his food and sat down at an open table, as all of the booths were taken.

Slightly attracted to the unusual personality Joshua possessed, Jennie set out on a mission to get to know him better, although in her mind, she wasn't quite sure.

Carrying her tray toward Joshua's table, as she approached it, she asked, "Do you mind if I sit here?"

Joshua didn't respond and Jennie took the seat anyway.

Jennie continued pressing what she believed previously was basically a one-way conversation.

She started by asking Joshua, "So, now that you don't have your face buried in a computer, are you going to tell me why you're going to Cheyenne?"

Joshua responded with a short question of his own, "Why do you want to know?"

"Because I'm a very determined person. When I set out to do something, I do it. It's the same thing when I want to know something. I don't stop until I find out what I want to know."

Joshua looked up at her and could tell the expression on her face certainly indicated that she meant what she just said.

Believing Jennie would not let up, Joshua decided to answer the question, "I'm looking for my parents."

Although he didn't believe so, Joshua may have finally met his match when it came to being stubborn, though both of them didn't perceive themselves as being stubborn, only determined.

"Where are your parents?" asked Jennie.

"If I knew that, I wouldn't be looking for them, would I?" Joshua responded in a snide manner.

Joshua finished his meal, and not wanting to be late getting back on the bus, he re-boarded before everyone else did. Jennie proceeded to do the same. The bus was still empty, and Joshua took the same seat next to the window toward the back of the bus. Jennie proceeded to sit down right next to him.

He looked up at her and said, "You know, you can have any seat you want. The bus is still empty."

Jennie responded, "I know. I want this one."

Joshua just looked away, opened his laptop, and continued to work on the program he was working on. The remaining passengers began to re-board. The bus was soon full again. The driver re-boarded the bus last, and now confident all the passengers had re-boarded, he took a seat and closed the door. The bus pulled out of the parking lot, headed back toward the interstate, and continued its journey north.

For now, Jennie was content to continue reading her book; however, she was quietly going over her plan to get Joshua to open up a little bit. Time passed, and Jennie attempted once again to initiate a conversation. She decided to ask Joshua what he was working on.

Joshua responded, "I'm working on a new computer program."

Jennie responded, "My uncle does computer programming. I'm told there is a lot more to it than people think."

"There is," responded Joshua, "The amount of commands that must be entered just to get the computer to do one small thing is staggering in itself." Joshua added, "Here, let me show you something I'm working on."

Jennie observed what he showed her, expressing interest and at the same time, thinking, "Finally."

Now that the ice had been broken, the two engaged in conversation off and on for the remainder of the trip.

Hours passed, and the driver made an announcement over the PA system, "We will be arriving in Fort Collins in about thirty minutes. A number of passengers will be disembarking in Fort Collins. We ask that all passengers who have a final destination of Fort Collins please check your seat and the area surrounding it, and be sure to have secured all your personal belongings."

Jennie looked at Joshua and said, "If you ever make it

back to Fort Collins, look me up." She handed Joshua a folded piece of paper and said, "Don't open that until after I leave."

Chapter 19

Just after Jennie got off the bus in Fort Collins, Joshua opened the folded piece of paper she had given him. Inside, there was only one word. It simply read "Jennie", followed by a seven-digit phone number, plus an area code. Joshua opened a new file and saved her number on his laptop, then he did something unusual. He reached in his back pocket, pulled out his wallet, and put the folded piece of paper in a zippered compartment of his wallet.

Time passed, and eventually the bus reached Cheyenne. The bus arrived at the station just after 1:30 AM, and Joshua needed to find a place to stay for the night. He asked the desk clerk if there was a Motel 17 nearby, and the desk clerk just said that he didn't know.

Joshua asked if they had Wi-Fi, and the desk clerk said, "Sure do."

Joshua opened up his laptop and searched for a Motel 17. He was surprised to learn that there was one just three blocks away. Joshua asked the desk clerk again if he could catch the city bus to the motel.

"Not this late," responded the desk clerk.

"Can I walk it?" asked Joshua.

"You can, but I wouldn't recommend it."

"Why?"

"'Cause this part of town ain't Cheyenne's best foot forward."

Knowing he had no other choice, Joshua just asked, "How do I get there?"

"Go out that door. Make a right. Walk three blocks, and

it'll be on your right. Not my first choice for a Motel 17, though."

Joshua started to walk toward the motel. No sooner than he had walked one block did the area in front of him light up in red, white, and blue lights. He heard a very short siren, and a spotlight was shining on him.

At the same time, these words were heard over a PA system, "Stop where you are. Put your hands behind your head."

Joshua complied, though he was very scared.

The officer's instructions continued, "Interlace your fingers. Walk backwards toward the sound of my voice. Stop. Get down on your knees. Spread your arms and legs."

The officer approached Joshua and said, "Give me your hand."

As the officer grabbed Joshua's hand and pulled upward, he said, "Pull up your knees."

When Joshua was standing, the officer pulled Joshua's other hand behind his back, cuffed him, and said, "You are not under arrest. This is just for my safety."

Next, the officer asked Joshua, "What are you doing in this part of town?"

"I just got off the bus."

"What bus?" asked the officer.

"At the bus station."

"Don't get smart with me. Where are you coming from?"

"I got on the bus in Sand City, Colorado."

"Do you have any ID on you?"

"Yes, it's in my wallet in my backpack."

"Do you have any weapons or anything else I need to know about?"

"I don't think so."

The officer patted Joshua down, searched his backpack, and retrieved his wallet. Upon looking at Joshua's ID, the first words out of his mouth were, "You're Joshua Fruskin?" in a voice that indicated some surprise to learn his identity.

"Yes."

Believing he was not in any imminent danger, the officer released Joshua from the handcuffs and asked, "What brings you to Cheyenne?"

"I'm looking for my parents."

"What makes you think your parents are in Cheyenne?"

"This is the last place that I know of where anyone saw them."

"Well, your parents' names are mighty well known around these parts. 'Specially by us folks in law enforcement. Can't say I'd be real proud of that name right now."

Joshua was upset by the officer's last statement, but didn't let it show. He asked the officer if he knew how to get to the Wyoming Department of Criminal Investigation. The officer told Joshua how to get there. Then he asked Joshua if he had a place to stay for the evening. Joshua said he was headed for the Motel 17 just down the street.

The officer said, "Get in. I'll take you. This isn't the best part of town."

Joshua got in the front seat of the passenger's side, and the officer dropped him off right in front of the door at the motel. Joshua walked up to the desk in the lobby, which was enclosed in glass. There was no one behind the desk, so he rang the bell on the counter. Once he did, a short girl, probably in her early twenties, with blonde hair and a ponytail approached the counter and asked if she could help him.

Joshua said he needed a room for the night, and the girl asked, "Just you?"

"Yes."

"Thirty-five, dollars plus a five dollar sheet deposit."

"What's a sheet deposit?"

"That's the price. Take it or leave it."

Joshua gave her the money, and she handed him a short form and said, "Fill this out."

Joshua did, and she handed him a card key and said, "Up the stairs, take a left, and it'll be down the hall on your right."

The room was just like the last one Joshua stayed in, but it had a dirty, grungy look to it. He didn't like the looks of the room, but he was tired. He just lied down on top of the bed, clothes and all, and fell asleep.

It wasn't long before morning came, and Joshua just wanted to get out of there. Aside from that, he was anxious to find some clues to his parents whereabouts. He turned the key in to the office and headed to a city bus stop. He remembered exactly what the officer said about how to get to the Wyoming Department of Criminal Investigation.

After a couple of bus transfers, Joshua arrived at his destination. When he walked inside the building, he discovered a very small lobby area with a window in the wall in front of him with a circular metal grate in it designed to allow for voice flow. There was a small slot at the bottom of the window to allow for paperwork to be passed through. There was a metal door to the right of the window.

Joshua walked up to the window, and an older lady, probably in her late-fifties, with very short hair and glasses, said, "May I help you?"

Joshua said, "I'm looking for my parents."

"Are they missing?"

"For over a month now."

"Have you filed a Missing Persons report?"

Joshua indicated that he had not, and the lady passed some paperwork through the slot in the window as she said, "Here, fill this out and hand it back to me."

Joshua picked up the pen and paper from the window. Not seeing chairs or a table, he took a seat on the floor and used his laptop as a desk.

Meanwhile, thinking not filling out a Missing Persons report for a month after disappearance was a little suspicious, the lady behind the counter took the opportunity to talk to a detective while Joshua was filling out the report. The detective thought it was suspicious as well and decided to review the report Joshua filled out.

After reading the report, the detective looked at Joshua

and said, "What is this, a joke? Look kid, filing a false Missing Persons report is a criminal offense."

Joshua replied, "It's not a false report. I'm Joshua Fruskin, and Steven and Fran Fruskin are my parents."

"Can you prove that?" asked the detective.

Joshua pulled his ID from his wallet and handed it to the detective through the slot in the window.

The detective looked at the ID, looked up at Joshua, and said, "In a minute, that door you see to the right of you is going to buzz. When it does, come on through."

Joshua followed the detective's instructions, and upon passing through the door, there was a hallway with cameras mounted on the walls pointing down towards him. At the end of the hallway, there was another door, this one metal, with a reinforced window in the top half. The detective Joshua had talked to was on the other side of the door to meet him, and he let Joshua in. The detective was of average height, about 5'8", had short black wavy hair, had a slightly dark complexion, and he spoke with an accent that Joshua found hard to understand.

The room was filled with desks. There were phones ringing, and it was slightly noisy. There was a bank of chairs against the wall.

The detective looked at Joshua as he pointed to the chairs and said, "Have a seat, young man."

Quite some time passed, and now Joshua was starting to become nervous. While Joshua was waiting patiently, the detective he originally talked to was on the phone with his supervisor. When the detective's supervisor learned that he had Joshua Fruskin on the premises, he instructed the detective to keep him there until he got back with him. After hanging up the phone, the detective's supervisor asked his secretary if the agent from the U.S. Department of Justice that was working on the Fruskin case was still available. The secretary said he was here this morning.

The detective's supervisor, a tall, bald man, in his mid-forties and dressed in a white shirt and tie, told the secretary, "Get him on the phone. Tell him it's urgent."

It wasn't long after that the secretary said, "I have Agent Benson on the phone."

The supervisor picked up his phone and said, "Agent Benson, this is Sargent Detective Supervisor Joe Sanders."

"How can I help you?" asked Agent Benson.

The Sargent continued, "I understand that you're still working on the Fruskin case."

"Sargent, I'm afraid all matters regarding that case are now under the jurisdiction of the Department of Justice. I'm afraid I can't divulge any information, Sargent."

"I'm not asking you to, Agent Benson. However, I believe I have some information that may be pertinent to your case."

"What do you have, Sargent?"

"We have a location of the whereabouts of one Joshua Fruskin."

"Sargent, the Department of Justice is fully aware of the location of Joshua Fruskin."

"I don't believe the information you have is current."

"What makes you say that?"

"Because we have Joshua downstairs."

"Sargent, in light of the current circumstances, I believe it might be best to discuss this matter in person."

The agent set up a meeting with Sargent Sanders within the hour.

When the agent met up with the sargent, their discussion continued as the agent told the sargent, "Sargent, I wanted to take the opportunity to talk to you in person because there are some factors in the Fruskin case you may not be aware of. Although Joshua Fruskin is not under investigation in this case, he is a person of interest, however, not in the usual definition of the term."

"Can you elaborate?" asked the Sargent.

"All I'm saying is you can't hold him."

"Agent Benson, this may be the break in the case you're looking for."

"Release him."

The Sargent reluctantly agreed to do as Agent Benson had asked, only because he had been instructed previously that the Department of Justice was heading up this investigation, and his department was to cooperate with the department in all matters concerning this investigation. However, the sargent had his own agenda with regards to this case. The sargent contacted the detective who originally told him Joshua Fruskin was on premises and told him to release Joshua.

So after waiting for over a couple of hours, and not knowing exactly what his fate would be, the same detective approached Joshua and said, "You're out of here, kid."

Joshua looked at the detective and said, "Excuse me?" in an attempt to verify what the detective had just said.

"You're free to go."

"So what about my parents?"

"We have your information, and if we learn anything, we'll contact you."

That wasn't good enough for Joshua, knowing this was the last law enforcement agency that had information concerning his parents.

"Who can I talk to about my parents?" asked Joshua.

The detective replied, "Look kid, I just told you. We have your information, and if we learn anything, we'll contact you." He continued, "You can't stay here," as he motioned Joshua toward the door where he originally let him in.

Frustrated, Joshua left, but he was still determined to find out the information he came for. He found a fast food chain where he could sit down with his laptop and utilize the free Wi-Fi to access the department's website again. Using the knowledge he had gained from his computer programming classes, he was able to hack into the department's public site through an e-mail form.

It took about an hour, but eventually he was able to access the administration information. A quick read of the files indicated how to access the department's intranet. Joshua saved that information to a hidden file and, knowing the amount of time it would take to access the department's database, elected to stay overnight at another Motel 17.

This Motel 17 was cleaner than the last one he stayed in, and he felt comfortable this time. Joshua set up his laptop on the table next to the window. Using the information in the hidden file, he accessed the department's computer again. Joshua programmed a Trojan to search the department's computers and send back copies of files that might be what he was looking for. Once that was done, Joshua programmed another Trojan virus to clear the command history of the previous one. Then he disconnected from the internet and proceeded to search the files he had copied.

It didn't take too long, and there it was, right in front of him. Once again, in blue lettering, "Case 378910 – Steven Fruskin, Fran Fruskin". Joshua clicked on it, and this time, there was a wealth of information that could help him in the search for his parents. In addition to the information Joshua had seen before, there was another section that read, "Montana State Police – U.S. Customs".

He clicked on that heading and read these words, "Montana State Police conducted an unfinished search of an RV on Interstate 94. MSP contacted U.S. Customs at the U.S./Canadian border. Inspectors found what they believed to be evidence of passengers. A subsequent interrogation of the driver revealed no further information."

Joshua returned to the previous page, and another heading caught his attention. This one read, "U.S. Department of Justice – Restricted access only". Joshua clicked on it and discovered yet another log-in screen. This piqued Joshua's interest, so he reviewed the hidden files he had copied, and with a little trial and error, he was able to access this page. The page had a U.S Department of Justice heading across the top. The page contained a huge list of names in alphabetical order. A little ways down the page, one of the lines read, "Fruskin, Steven – Fran". Joshua clicked on it, and there was a heading that read "Credible Information". Below that, it read "Last Known Location: Custody of Canadian Border Services Agency". Below that was basically a repeat of the information that was obtained by the Wyoming Department of Criminal Investigation, so Joshua put two and two together and realized that his parents had crossed the Canadian border.

Joshua did a little more research on the computer and discovered he did not need a U.S. passport to enter Canada. A passport was only necessary to return. He had a strong gut feeling that his parents were in Canada, so he made plans to go to the bus station tomorrow and buy another ticket, this time to the closest border town he could find. For now, it was time to get some rest, so Joshua turned in for the evening. Morning came and Joshua made his way back to the bus station. When he arrived, he discovered the same man behind the counter as when he first arrived.

Joshua's first thought was to try and compute the time he was gone and the possible shifts the man could work but realized it would center around what the man was scheduled, and aside from that, he was here to buy a bus ticket. He explained that he needed to get as close to Canada as he could.

The man responded, "We don't offer service to Canada."

Joshua responded, "That's not what I said. I need to get as close to Canada as I can. How far north do you go?"

"Hmm, let me see here. I can get you as far as Shoring, Montana. That's about twenty miles from the border. No bus stations there though. Just a gas station."

"How much?"

"One way or round trip?"

"One way."

The man quoted the price, and Joshua purchased the ticket. The bus didn't leave for a couple of hours, and Joshua decided to work on the computer program he was working on again. As he began to work on the computer, he couldn't help but feel like somebody was watching him. He looked behind him but didn't see anybody that appeared to be watching him, so he continued working on the computer.

Time passed, and eventually Joshua heard over the loudspeaker the announcement of departure that by now had become all to familiar, "Bus 47 with service to Wheatland; Casper; Buffalo; Sheridan; Billings, Montana; Lewistown; Malta; and Shoring now boarding at gate two. All ticketed passengers, please board now."

Joshua closed up his laptop, gathered his belongings, and boarded the bus. It was practically empty, and Joshua took a seat next to the window toward the back of the bus. Several passengers boarded, and it wasn't long before the bus pulled out of the station. This time, Joshua was glad to have an empty seat next to him, knowing he could concentrate on his work without interruption. As the bus made its way out of Cheyenne and onto the interstate, Joshua had that same feeling he had earlier, as though someone was watching him. He didn't look behind him this time, instead, he continued with his work.

A little more time passed, and Joshua reached a stopping point in his work. He closed his laptop and watched the scenery pass him by out the window. He looked at the empty seat next to him, and his thoughts turned to Jennie. He actually missed her. Hours passed, and eventually, the bus arrived in Shoring. It pulled into the parking lot of a small convenience store, and at this point, Joshua and one other person were the only ones on the bus.

The driver announced a short announcement over the PA that was just one word, "Shoring."

Joshua and the man that was sitting toward the back of the bus both exited, as did the driver, in order to retrieve suitcases. Joshua only had his backpack, which he carried with him, so he went into the convenience store in an effort to find further transportation to the Canadian border. The man that got off the bus with him only retrieved a small duffel bag and followed Joshua into the convenience store. The convenience store was old, not very well lit, and had wood shelves that were stocked with very little merchandise.

Joshua asked the man behind the counter how he could get to the Canadian border.

"From here?" the man asked in a voice that seemed to sound as though he believed it were impossible.

Meanwhile, Joshua was thinking to himself that that had to be one of the stupidest questions he had ever heard. He responded, "Of course from here, where else?"

The man looked at Joshua with a silent pause for a minute and then responded, "I suppose you could walk north of town and then thumb it."

"Thumb it?" Joshua repeated back to the man in the form of a question that indicated he didn't understand the man's answer.

"You know, cop a ride, or what do you younger folks call it? Never mind, plain English, I'd just call it like it is, hitchhike."

"Isn't that dangerous?"

"From where I'm standing, I don't see you have much of a choice."

Joshua left and began walking on the main street, heading north out of town. The man that had followed him into the convenience store asked the man behind the counter where the local police station was.

The man responded, "Sheriff's office is across the street." With that, the man left the convenience store and headed across the street.

Meanwhile, after walking about twenty minutes, Joshua thought he was far enough out of town to where he could try his hand at hitchhiking for the first time, although he was very apprehensive about doing so. Not wanting to do anything illegal, he continued to walk north alongside the road. However, after a while, he began to get tired and started to rationalize that hitchhiking, although dangerous, wasn't a very serious crime. Though, when he looked behind him, the road was void of cars, so he continued walking. Time passed, and he saw one car, but when he held up his thumb in hope of a ride, the car passed him by. As he continued walking, he grew even more tired, and began to hold his thumb up only when he heard a car, and without looking back, which was a very unusual move for Joshua. After not hearing another car for quite some time, Joshua finally heard one in the distance. He held his thumb up again.

The car pulled up alongside Joshua, and a deep local voice asked, "Where you headed, son?"

As Joshua looked to his left, he saw that the man behind the voice was a heavy set man, in his late-forties, wearing a western hat and a law enforcement uniform that matched it. The two-way radio and the computer in front of the center dash were all Joshua needed to confirm that this was an unmarked patrol car. The man in the passenger's seat was the same man that was on the bus with him and who had followed him into the convenience store a few miles back.

The man in the passenger's seat said, "Joshua, my name is Agent Benson. I've been following your parents' case for some time. Get in, and we'll talk about it.

Joshua got in the back seat, sat down, and asked Agent Benson, "You know where my parents are?"

Agent Benson answered, "We believe they're in the custody of the Canadian Government." As the patrol car continued north, the conversation continued with Agent Benson taking the lead, "Joshua, as an agent of the U.S. Department of Justice, it is my duty to inform you that the U.S. Department of Justice does not feel that it would be in your best interest, or the Department's for that matter, if you were to cross the border. However, at this point, we have no legal recourse to stop you, should you choose to do so."

"What will happen if I cross the border?"

"The U.S. Government cannot guarantee your safety, or your safe return to the U.S., for that matter."

In the distance up ahead, Joshua could see a small building on the right with a U.S. flag flying next to it and a small parking lot beside the building.

Chapter 20

As the patrol car pulled into the parking lot of the tiny U.S. Customs building, Joshua told Agent Benson, "That's okay. I understand. Now let me out."

The sheriff exited the driver's seat, walked around the front of the vehicle to the back door where Joshua was sitting, opened the door, and let Joshua out. Joshua walked into the tiny U.S. Customs office, which was staffed by a single agent. Joshua asked the agent if he needed a passport to enter Canada.

The agent, a young girl in her early twenties, answered Joshua's question with, "Not to enter, but you will need to present it to Customs upon your return. Do you have your passport with you?"

"I don't have one," replied Joshua.

"I cannot stop you from entering Canada without a passport, however, I strongly discourage it. You cannot re-enter the U.S. without proper documentation. You may be able to obtain a passport from the U.S. consulate in Canada. However, proof of citizenship and proper documentation are required, and it is not a simple process."

Joshua looked outside the window of the door he had just came through, and saw the unmarked patrol car still waiting in the parking lot. Joshua walked out the door and continued walking up the road to the north toward the Canadian border. As he continued north, eventually he saw a faded sign that read, "Leaving USA. Stop and report to Canadian Customs".

Joshua walked into the Canadian Customs building. The border agent asked to see Joshua's passport. Joshua said he didn't have one, and the agent then asked for a state issued ID or driver's license.

Joshua showed the agent his ID, and the agent looked at Joshua and said, "Just a minute."

As the agent picked up the phone, he told Joshua to have a seat. Joshua couldn't quite hear what the man was saying, but, if his past experiences were any indication of the immediate future, he had a very good idea of what to expect next.

The border agent hung up the phone and said to Joshua, "Just hang tight for a few minutes."

Sure enough, just a few minutes went by, and two Royal Canadian Mounted Police patrol cars pulled into the parking lot. The mounties exited their vehicles and began to walk toward the Customs office door.

Both of the mounties came inside, and one looked at Joshua and said, "Joshua Fruskin?"

Joshua looked up and said, "Yes."

The Mountie asked him to stand up. When he did, the Mountie pulled back his arm behind him.

As he put on the handcuffs, he said, "Joshua, you are not under arrest. This is just for my safety."

Those words had now become somewhat familiar to Joshua.

The Mountie took a moment and patted Joshua down, then said, "Would you come with me, please?"

He and the other Mountie walked out of the Customs building and led Joshua to the back of the patrol car. The Mountie removed the cuffs and told Joshua to have a seat in the back of his patrol car. The mounties took a minute to talk to each other in front of the patrol cars. The Mountie that took Joshua to his car returned to it and took a seat behind the wheel. Joshua just sat quietly in the back of the car, a little scared and not knowing what was going to happen next.

As the Mountie started the car, he began to speak as he looked in the rear-view mirror in an effort to make eye contact with Joshua, "Joshua, you are not under arrest. However, under the direction of Canada's Minister of Public Safety, you are being placed in protective custody."

"I just want to find my parents," replied Joshua.

The Mountie took Joshua into the small town of Elkmont. When they arrived at the station, the Mountie walked to the back of the patrol car, opened the door for Joshua, and walked him inside the station. He continued to escort Joshua to a small office and opened the door for Joshua. Inside the office, there was a man behind a desk who motioned for the Mountie to close the door, thus leaving Joshua inside the office alone with the man.

The man looked at Joshua and said, "Sit down, Joshua." He continued, "Joshua, I'm Jeff Monarch, director for the CBSA. I have already had the pleasure of meeting your parents."

"You know where my parents are?" asked Joshua.

"I'm afraid I don't," replied Jeff. "I do know they are in the custody of the Canadian Government."

Joshua just looked down toward the floor, frustrated that his journey had taken him this far, and yet, he felt as though he was no closer to finding his parents.

Jeff continued to speak, "I've been instructed to have you transported to the station in Reibers. I wish I could tell you more, however, my supervisors tell me this case is being handled on a need-to-know basis." He paused for a moment, then said, "I don't want you to stay where your parents stayed when they were here. There is a break room down the hall. There are some vending machines and a table and some chairs. You will be leaving for Reibers this evening."

Jeff picked up the phone and summoned one of his mounties to his office to escort Joshua to the break room. When Joshua walked into the break room, he saw a table and chairs on the left, a bank of vending machines on the right, and a counter with a sink, microwave, and coffeemaker against the far wall. There was a small refrigerator under the counter. One of the vending machines was the refrigerated type, and it offered sandwiches and fruit as some of its choices. Joshua had convinced himself that the American coins he had would not work in Canadian vending machines, but his hunger had got the best of him. In an unusual move for him, Joshua decided to try the American coins, and to his surprise, the vending machine accepted them. He was able to get himself a sandwich and coke. Joshua worked on his laptop for a while, but he was not able to get online.

A couple of hours went by, and eventually a Mountie entered the break room and said, "Joshua Fruskin?" although he already knew the answer to his own question.

Joshua answered, "Yes, sir."

"I'm officer Friedmont. I've been instructed to provide you transportation to the city of Reibers."

"Why are we going to Reibers?"

"All I can tell you is I've been instructed to transport you to the city of Reibers to facilitate further transportation."

"Further transportation to where?"

"I'm afraid I don't have any information with regards to where you'll be going after you are transported to Reibers." Officer Friedmont escorted Joshua to his patrol car and opened the rear door behind the driver's seat for him.

Joshua took a seat and officer Friedmont took a seat behind the driver's seat. Upon arriving at the station in Reibers, officer Friedmont escorted Joshua into the station and to the office of Brian Anderson, Vice President of Enforcement for the CBSA. When Joshua entered the office, he saw four chairs against the wall on the right and a desk in the center of the room on the left. Behind the desk was a tall man, in his mid-fifties, with a short hair cut, wearing a well-tailored suit.

He looked at Joshua and said, "Sit down, Joshua."

Joshua took a seat and just looked down at the ground, as he was scared to death not knowing what was going to happen next.

The man behind the desk began to speak again, saying, "Joshua, I'm Brian Anderson, Vice President of Enforcement for the CBSA. I understand you're concerned about your parents' whereabouts"

"Yes, sir," Joshua responded in a very quite sheepish voice, without looking up.

"I can certainly tell you that your parents are safe."

"If you know they're safe, then you know where they are," Joshua replied in a frustrated voice.

"Joshua, I'm afraid your parents' case is being handled on a need-to-know basis, and your last statement is inaccurate."

"Who does know where they are?"

"Joshua, I'm acting under the direction of Jason Culver. Jason is Canada's Minister of Public Safety, and his office is responsible for overseeing virtually every law enforcement agency in Canada."

"So what does that mean for me?"

"It means, I believe, you're going to see your parents very soon." Brian continued his conversation with Joshua, "Joshua, my instructions are to provide you transportation to the airport in Reibers and ensure that you board a specifically designated nonstop flight to the city of Ottawa, where you will be met at the gate, in Ottawa, by agents from the office of the Minster of Public Safety."

"What happens after that?"

"I'm afraid I can't provide you with any more information than that."

"Why?" Joshua asked in a manner that was indicative of the way he would usually ask when he intended to ask a specific line of questions that would eventually provide him the information he was seeking.

Brian's answer would not fulfill Joshua's intentions, though, specifically because he could not answer with the substance Joshua anticipated. He truly did not have the information Joshua was looking for. He had been completely honest with Joshua, as Joshua's parents' case was truly being handled on a need-to-know basis at the direction of Jason Culver's office.

Brian replied to Joshua's question, "Joshua, as I said earlier, your parents' case is being handled on a need-to-know basis, and I simply don't have that information."

Brian picked up the phone and summoned two mounties that he himself had specifically chosen to ensure Joshua would not only get to the airport in Reibers, but also specifically board the plane he was intended to board. The mounties escorted Joshua to an awaiting patrol car, and one of them opened the rear door behind the driver's seat. Joshua got in, and the Mountie shut the door and then took a seat behind the wheel while the other Mountie got into the front passenger's seat. The ride to the airport was short, and Joshua didn't say anything on the way there.

The mounties escorted Joshua through the airport, through security, and right to the gate. They both stayed with him until the flight was boarded and ensured he walked down the catwalk to the plane. The flight took two and a half hours, and Joshua was very happy to learn a meal was being served on this flight. After eating a box lunch consisting of a sandwich, pretzels, an apple, and yogurt, Joshua used the remaining time on the flight to sleep.

Joshua was awakened from his cat nap by these words, "Ladies and gentlemen, this is your captain. We are beginning our descent to the city of Ottowa, where the temperature is currently eighteen degrees Celsius. For those of you less familiar with our temperature scale, that would be about 65 degrees Fahrenheit. At this time, we would ask that you please look around your seats to ensure that you do not leave any of your personal belongings behind. Your flight attendant will be by your seat to collect any trash you might have. We should be landing in Ottowa in less than thirty minutes. As your captain, I wanted to take this opportunity to personally thank you for flying Canadian Airlines."

The plane was prepared for landing, and as Joshua looked out the window, he could see the city below him come into view. It wasn't long after that the plane landed and taxied to the tarmac and to the gate. When Joshua got to the top of the catwalk, there were two men standing facing the catwalk. The two both were wearing suits and looked as though they could be agents from the U.S. Secret Service. Joshua stopped for the moment and both men flashed an ID.

One of them said, "Joshua Fruskin?"

Joshua didn't say anything, and the man continued to speak, "Joshua, I'm Agent Freiss. I work out of the office of Canada's Minister of Public Safety. I've been directed to provide you with further transportation."

Joshua answered the agent with, "Can I see your ID again?"

"Certainly," replied Agent Freiss.

As the agent showed Joshua his ID again, Joshua continued, "Would you just pull it out?"

Right about now, agent Friess was becoming slightly miffed with what he perceived to be Joshua's lack of manners; however, he compiled. As Joshua studied the ID, he asked how he could be sure it was real.

The agent replied, "Trust me. It's real, kid, but I admire your attention to detail," and agent Freiss pointed out the holographic images on his ID.

When Joshua was satisfied the ID was real, he looked at the other agent and said, "Can I see yours?"

The other agent just looked at agent Freiss for a moment. Agent Friess just nodded his head in an indication for the other agent to comply with Joshua's request. Once Joshua was convinced that both ID's were valid, he agreed to go with them, although both agents were well aware that Joshua had no choice in the matter.

"Are we going to see my parents?" asked Joshua.

Agent Freiss replied, "I'm afraid, at the moment, I am not at liberty to provide you with that information," as they walked through the airport.

Joshua was always very observant, and when he put two and two together, he was usually right. So when the three of them passed by the escalators that led to ground transportation and the baggage area, Joshua knew that he was most likely about to get on another plane. The agents led Joshua to another gate, but this time they both accompanied him through. This gate consisted of a staircase that led down to the tarmac. Outside on the tarmac was an awaiting helicopter.

Agent Freiss and his partner led Joshua to the helicopter, and agent Freiss motioned for Joshua to get in. Once Joshua climbed aboard, agent Friess boarded as well. For the moment, this seemed to be where he and his partner parted ways.

Agent Freiss handed Joshua a headset and said, "Here, put this on."

Joshua held the headset in his hands for a minute as he watched the pilot and agent Freiss put their headsets on. As the pilot reached above to a control panel, Joshua watched with keen interest in what the pilot was doing. Just afterward, he could hear the whine and rev of the helicopter engines and rotors as they both began to reach the level needed for takeoff.

Joshua put the headset on, and it wasn't too much longer before the copter was in the air. The view from the helicopter was so much different from the view from the plane. Joshua could see the city below him at a much closer distance. It wasn't long before the helicopter was out of the city, and the landscape began to change.

Joshua began to hear the voice of agent Freiss over the headset he was wearing, "Joshua, As I told you earlier at the airport when you asked me if we were going to see your parents, at that moment, I was not at liberty to provide you with that information. Joshua, first of all, I want you to understand something. Your parents' case is a very sensitive issue for the Canadian Government. How we handle every issue connected with this case could have a direct effect on U.S. and Canadian relations. That being said, everything involving this case is not only being handled on a need-to-know basis, but much of the information surrounding this case is being handled covertly. What I need from you, Joshua, is your assurance that the Canadian Government will have your full cooperation when it comes to anything concerning this case."

"I just want to see my parents," replied Joshua.

"Well, Joshua, that's what we're about to do."

The flight took about forty-five minutes, and eventually

the helicopter landed in a clearing in the woods. During the course of the flight, Agent Freiss instructed Joshua on what the Canadian Government was asking of him, including the need to keep his identity a secret, except to those that were directly involved in his parents' case. When they landed, they were met by another agent of the office of Canada's Minister of Public Safety. Agent Freiss explained to Joshua that this agent was here to provide ground transportation to Joshua's destination. Joshua reasoned in his mind that his destination was to find his parents, and interpreted Agent Freiss's statement as a confirmation that he was going to see his parents. As soon as Joshua exited the helicopter, it took off again, with Agent Freiss still on board.

The man on the ground identified himself as Agent Preston and only said, "Come with me."

Joshua complied based on what agent Freiss had told him, and the two walked a short distance through the woods to an awaiting car. The car was a small, silver, four-door sedan. It was a later model, and when Joshua got in, this time in the front passenger's seat at Agent Preston's direction, he could see no evidence that this car was any type of a government vehicle. Now, with a slight question in his mind where they were going, Joshua just remained quiet. The trip was a short one, and the two of them drove through town and eventually arrived at a two-story, cedar-sided cabin just outside of town.

They were met at the car by a man who identified himself as Jeff Laskin. Agent Preston told Joshua to accompany Jeff. Joshua was apprehensive about getting out, but something in his mind was telling him to do as Agent Preston asked.

Once inside, there, standing in the living room, was the whole purpose for his trip, all three of them. Joshua immediately ran to his mother and hugged her. Then, after what was an unusually long hug for Joshua, he did the same for his dad. Steven wasn't much for long hugs, but he sensed this one was very important to Joshua, and he let Joshua determine what was long enough this time. As Joshua looked at Justin,

Justin put both hands in the air in front of him, in an effort to indicate there was no need to hug him. That didn't stop Joshua, and the two embraced in a short hug that only reinforced what Justin already knew, his older brother loved him very much. The four of them spent the rest of the evening catching up.

When Steven and Justin relayed to Joshua some of the experiences they had been through, Joshua questioned the validity of some of their statements. This was nothing unusual for Joshua, and it sparked some arguments between Joshua and Steven, a situation which was all too common when the four of them were living together. It was something that Fran despised with a passion. Nevertheless, the evening came to a close, and the four of them retired for the night.

Morning came, and when Joshua came downstairs into the living room, Steven and Justin, and some guy Joshua had never seen before were all in the room. Joshua just looked at Steven with an expression that could only mean, "Who is this man?"

Steven answered Joshua's silent question, "Joshua, this is David Bryar. He and the gentleman you met last night take turns watching over us in twelve-hour shifts." Steven continued, "Agent Bryar has been instructed to provide you with a debriefing."

"What's a debriefing?" Joshua asked his dad.

Agent Bryar answered, "A debriefing is a conversation that is held with an individual or individuals after they have been through a chain of events and is intended to provide those individuals with direction on what or what not to do with information they have acquired. In your case, Joshua, this debriefing is intended just for you."

Steven looked at Joshua and said, "It's okay, Joshua. You're just going to the kitchen."

When Agent Bryar and Joshua were safely out of earshot of the others, Agent Bryar began to speak again, "Joshua, I'm very happy you were finally able to find you parents. However, as you've been told before, your parents' case is a very sensitive one, as far as the Canadian Government is concerned. That being said, the information you were exposed to last night in the course of conversation with you family could have very serious consequences for the Canadian Government if it were provided to the wrong people. As a result, I've been instructed to allow you to remain a guest of the Canadian Government."

"You mean I can't go anywhere," Joshua replied in what was obviously a statement and not a question.

"Please do not interpret this action as being held against your will. We intend to make your stay with us as pleasant as possible, just as we have done for your parents and brother."

Chapter 21

As the days passed, unbeknownst to Steven, Fran, Joshua, and Justin, the Canadian Government and the U.S government were active in a negotiation process that was intended to result in an amicable solution for both countries. The stumbling block was Canada's determination to protect the interest of Steven, Fran, and Justin. As negotiations progressed, the U.S. Department of Justice insisted that the three be returned to the U.S. and prosecuted for crimes committed, as well as undergo trial in federal courts for matters concerning U.S. national security. A representative from Canada's Department of Foreign Affairs, at the same time, was insisting that his government would not allow that.

The representative, a taller man in his late-fifties, rather thin in appearance, who obviously aged well, began to speak and address a small group of officials from both the U.S. Department of Justice and Canada's Department of Foreign Affairs, "Gentlemen, as I'm sure you already know, the Canadian Government's position on this matter is a direct result of our investigations on matters surrounding this case."

A representative from the U.S. Department of Justice answered, "How is it your investigation results in Canada's refusal to extradite three citizens of the United States for prosecution of crimes that were committed in the United States?"

"Our government's investigation revealed that these crimes were committed as an act of necessity, and all three were acting on the belief that any contact with law enforcement in the U.S. would only result in a direct threat to their safety. A conclusion that the Canadian Government is inclined to agree with."

A spokesman for the U.S. Department of Justice replied, "How is the Canadian Government's investigation of this case able to reveal that these crimes were allegedly committed as an act of necessity?"

The Canadian representative answered, "Mr. Spokesman, we are all aware that both of our governments do whatever is necessary in order to ensure the national security of our countries, which certainly includes ensuring that our countries are portrayed in a manner to the rest of the world that is consistent with our past."

The spokesman for the U.S. Department of Justice answered the Canadian representative, "Would you care to elaborate on that statement?"

"No, I would not," replied the Canadian representative.

Another member of the U.S. Department of Justice also began to speak, "I would like to take this opportunity to address Canada's Minister of Public Safety regarding the events surrounding this case."

Canada's representative nodded in agreement, and the man began what was obviously going to be a line of questioning designed to implicate Canada's alleged misconduct in handling matters involved in this case, "Mr. Culver, would I be correct in my assumption that your office was directly responsible for the whereabouts of Steven Fruskin, Fran Fruskin, and Justin Fruskin once they had crossed Canada's border?"

Mr. Culver responded, "Once our office learned that the three of them had crossed the border and were in the custody of the CBSA, our office initiated the procedures necessary to ensure that we were constantly aware of the three's whereabouts."

The U.S. spokesman responded with, "Mr. Culver, am I to assume that by that statement that your government was already tracking the whereabouts of Steven, Fran, and Justin Fruskin while they were still in the United States?"

"I'm afraid I am not at liberty to answer that question."

"Then who is?"

"I believe I can answer that question," a spokesman for the Federal Bureau of Investigation with the U.S. delegation answered and continued to speak. "First of all, let me reiterate what has been made publicly known in the past by myself and many others in positions similar to the one I hold. It is not uncommon for countries to work together in the course of an investigation for any case where it may be deemed necessary to do so. That being said, our agency was actively sharing information with those foreign agencies that we believed would be in a position to accomplish the objectives of our agency."

"And what would those objectives be?" asked Canada's representative.

The FBI representative answered, "To best protect the interest of the U.S. Government and matters of U.S. national security. Our objective was to locate and detain Steven, Fran, and Justin Fruskin until a determination could be made on what course of action would be in the best interest of the United States national security."

The Canadian representative answered the FBI representative, "Mr. Spokesman, I understand that your position is to uphold the constitution and the laws of the United States, and you were sworn to do that. Would that be a fair statement?"

The spokesman for the FBI answered, "It is my responsibility to ensure that laws are enforced in a manner that would safeguard the principles of our constitution."

The Canadian representative answered, "Does not that same constitution provide for the fair and consistent treatment of all citizens of the United States, including those of Steven, Fran, and Justin Fruskin?"

The FBI agent answered with a more candid and less politically correct answer, "I know where you're going. My responsibility is to protect the interest of the United States government. There are times when we are forced to make the hard decisions and choose the option that would best serve that objective."

The Canadian representative answered with a question, "Even if it involves the total disregard for a fair and equitable resolution to those who are in the direct path to receive the effects of what I would, and I believe the Canadian Government would, interpret as a great miscarriage of justice?"

The FBI spokesman answered, "I believe I have already answered your question in the course of the previous statements."

The Canadian representative answered, "I believe you have. I also want you to understand that our government is a party to protecting the best interest of Canadian law-abiding citizens. The results of our investigation revealed that Steven, Fran, and Justin were what would traditionally be what both of our countries would consider law-abiding citizens until the actions of the U.S. Government forced them to do otherwise. That being said, my government believes that our country is under a moral obligation to protect the interest of these three."

The FBI representative responded with, "Mr. Spokesman, may I remind you that Steven, Fran, and Justin Fruskin are not Canadian citizens, however? They are citizens of the United States, and therefore, subject to the laws of the United States."

The Canadian spokesman answered, "That can be resolved."

The FBI representative answered, "Is that a threat?"

A spokesperson for the U.S. Department of Justice chimed in, "Gentlemen, we are here to determine what is in the best interest of both of our countries. I suggest that our conversations take a path that will lead to that objective."

Chapter 22

The negotiations continued with the same political rhetoric that one would expect would occur when two governments attempt to hash out a solution to what they both perceived to be a problem, and both countries had the intention of coming out on top regarding the issue.

***

As time passed, Susan, Joshua's grandmother was becoming rather concerned with Joshua's whereabouts, as he was only supposed to be gone two weeks. It had now been longer, and she had not heard from him. She made phone call after phone call in an attempt to locate Joshua and only met with minimal success. The last place Susan could determine and confirm Joshua had been was Cheyenne, Wyoming. When she talked to the agent at the bus station in Cheyenne, she asked if Joshua had purchased a ticket to travel anywhere else. The agent answered that he was not at liberty to provide that information.

Susan responded to that statement in her usual assertive manner, "Look young man, I don't care what you are at liberty or not at liberty to tell me. What *I* am at liberty to tell you is that if you don't tell me where my grandson went next, you can bet your bottom dollar that, in no short order, you can expect to see me walk into that bus station of yours, and I promise you this. I will find out where Joshua went next if it kills me. Now, unless you want to see that happen, and I don't believe you do, I suggest you tell me where my grandson went next."

Not wanting to continue this conversation any further, the bus station agent responded, "Look lady, I can see that this is very important to you, so I'm going to go out on a limb here and tell you that your grandson bought a ticket to Shoring, Montana. I can't tell you any more than that."

With that information in hand, Susan was able to determine the last place Joshua had been was the small border town of Shoring, Montana. She didn't know where Joshua had gone from there, but she had a strong gut feeling that he had crossed the border.

The very next day, late in the evening, Susan heard a car drive up her gravel driveway. As she looked outside, she could see two men getting out of the car. Susan got up to answer the door before either of the men had a chance to knock. The man who got out of the passenger's seat identified himself as Agent Benson with the U.S. Department of Justice and asked Joshua's grandmother if she was indeed Susan Giddings.

Susan answered, "Who wants to know?"

Agent Benson responded, "Well, ma'am, I do. May I come in please?"

"Do you have some identification?"

Agent Benson allowed Susan to see the identification she requested and she let the two men in.

Once they were inside, Agent Benson continued his conversation, "Now that you have had an opportunity to see my identification, may I please see yours? Because if you are, in fact, Susan Giddings, I have some information that I believe you would consider very important."

"What information?" asked Susan.

"Ma'am, your ID please?"

Susan produced the ID, and Agent Benson told Susan, "Mrs. Giddings, I believe we have information concerning the last known whereabouts of your grandson, and we need to know if he has made contact with you since then."

"What exactly do you mean by the last known whereabouts?"

"Ma'am, we can only confirm that Joshua crossed the U.S./Canadian border north of Shoring, Montana, but as far as tracking his whereabouts after crossing the border, I can only say we have limited information."

"What limited information?"

"Ma'am, because of matters involving U.S. national security, I'm afraid I can't answer that."

Joshua's grandmother responded, "Oh, yes you can and will answer my question."

Agent Benson just handed Susan a card and said, "Mrs. Giddings, if you hear from your grandson, please contact me. I cannot stress enough how imperative it is that you only contact myself with any information you may receive. Please do not divulge what you have learned or learn in the future, including our conversation today, with any one else in the agency or, for that matter, any other law enforcement agency."

As the two of them drove away, Susan took the opportunity to write down the plate number. She had no intention of letting the conversation she just had sway her from her efforts to find her grandson. As time passed, she continued to run into brick walls in her efforts, as all of the contacts she was making were agencies of the Canadian Government. In an act of desperation, she retrieved the card Agent Benson had given her and contacted him directly, as she had been asked to do.

As soon as Agent Benson answered the phone, and Susan was absolutely positive this was his voice, she said, "So, have you found my grandson, yet?"

Agent Benson replied, "I'm afraid we don't have any further leads, however, I believe you can be of some help in the case."

"Oh, I can, can I?"

"Mrs. Giddings, I believe I would be able to help you in a fashion that would be acceptable to you if I just had your full cooperation."

"Agent Benson, it's not your grandson who is missing."

"I understand that, and I can assure you that our

department is doing everything within its power to bring your grandson home. However, I believe you are in a position to help us do that."

"How so, Agent Benson?"

"I'd like to take the opportunity to discuss that with you in person."

"Okay, Agent Benson. I can talk to you..."

Agent Benson cut her off, "Mrs. Giddings, our agency is fully aware of what time or times are most convenient for you," and he preceded to hang up the phone.

The very next day, late in the evening, once again, Susan heard a car drive up her driveway. When she looked out the window, she saw that it was Agent Benson, although, this time he did not have anybody with him.

Susan opened the door for him and said, "So what do you want to talk about?" as the agent still stood at the door.

Agent Benson calmly spoke, "Mrs. Giddings, may I come in, please?"

Susan just stood back and opened the door wide as if to say, "Come on in" in a manner that manifested frustration, though she said nothing.

Once Agent Benson was inside, he continued his conversation, "Mrs. Giddings, whether you choose to believe it or not, you and I are working towards the same goal, and that is to bring your grandson back to the United States."

Susan answered, "Well, I don't see much progress from your office in that department."

"Susan, that's where I need your assistance. We need to enlist the help of Canadian citizens in attempting to locate your grandson."

"And what about my daughter, son-in-law, and other baby?"

"I believe what I am about to ask you to do could very well give us the edge we need in locating all of them."

"And just what is it you intend on asking me to do?" Susan asked in the usual assertive manner that, by now, Agent Benson had become all too familiar with.

Agent Benson replied, "Mrs. Giddings, what I'm about to ask you to do may be deemed inappropriate by certain individuals who's interest may not be exactly aligned with the common interest the two of us share. With that in mind, if you choose to go forward with the agenda that I am about to propose to you, it is the utmost necessity that if your actions are questioned in any manner, no matter where those questions may originate, there must absolutely not be any mention made of conversation with myself or anyone else from the Department of Justice."

Susan looked at Agent Benson with kind of a stare that only could be described as the look of a question mark.

Agent Benson continued, "What I need you to do is to arrange a meeting with a reporter from one of your local affiliated TV stations. My guess is that when they learn of your situation, they will be all too quick to air your story as a matter of human interest, something that usually drives ratings."

Susan asked, "Agent Benson, how is a small human interest story ran by a local TV station going to bring my grandson back to the U.S.?"

"You just leave the rest to me, Mrs. Giddings. I can assure you that your efforts will by no means be without significance."

Chapter 23

In the days that followed, Susan did exactly as Agent Benson asked. The local station was all too interested in Mrs. Giddings story and did not hesitate at all in airing it. In no short order, the story was picked up by its national affiliate, and in the weeks that followed a number of news magazines, and programs. As the letters and phone calls poured in, Susan was beginning to question her decision to follow Agent Benson's directions. What Susan was about to learn next would only confirm that.

Just as she was about to take a moment to try and relax in the hopes of relieving the stress brought on by recent events, the beginning of *The World Around Us*, one of the many news magazine shows began its broadcast, "And do you remember this grandmother's plea to bring her daughter, grandsons, and son-in-law home? Well, you won't believe what our undercover investigation has revealed."

Susan watched with great interest, and as the show progressed, her story began to air.

Watching herself on TV, she listened as the reporter said, "Recently, we aired a human interest story where this grandmother issued a public plea to bring her daughter, grandsons, and son-in-law home. At the same time the story aired, it was believed that the four may have crossed the border into Canada, and this grandmother was asking for the help of both U.S. and Canadian citizens in locating her family in a desperate attempt to ensure their safe return home. Well, what our undercover investigation has revealed is that public plea may have had just the opposite effect on that objective. We go now to our special investigative reporter, Frank Maynard, for additional details."

Frank Maynard continued, "Well, John, what *The World Around Us* has learned is that while this public plea was being issued, picked up, and aired by national affiliates, the U.S. and Canada were already in high levels of negotiations in an attempt to return Steven Fruskin, Fran Fruskin, Justin Fruskin, and now even Joshua Fruskin home. *The World Around Us* has learned that the U.S. Department of Justice was heading up these negotiations. Although no one from the Department of Justice would agree to speak to us publicly, we did manage to find someone within the department who would only agree to talk with us off-camera and on the condition he spoke with us anonymously. The insider stated that the United States was holding the position that Steven, Fran, and Justin Fruskin be returned to the U.S. to face prosecution for crimes committed in the United States. John, I want to be very clear here and point out that Joshua Fruskin is not facing any charges, and as far as we know, Joshua has not committed any alleged crimes in the U.S. or Canada. The stumbling block here is that the Canadian Government feels that the crimes allegedly committed by these three in the U.S. were done so as an act of necessity and fear that their safety was in jeopardy if the three were to have any contact with the U.S. law enforcement."

John asked Fran, "Frank, did these three have any previous record prior to the events that recently took place?"

"John, that question puts an interesting spin on things. Earlier in the year, all three major networks had reported that Steven Fruskin and Fran Fruskin had both escaped from two separate medium-security prisons in the western part of New Mexico. Our investigation has revealed that story to be absolutely false, although all three major networks insist that the information they were provided with came from very credible sources. As far as we can tell, Steven, Fran, and even Justin Fruskin were all very much law-abiding citizens prior to all of this taking place. And, John, that is the reason for

Canada's hesitation to comply with the U.S. request."

"Frank, are these three, or for that matter, four, in the custody of the Canadian Government?"

"At this point, I would say that would be a fair assumption, although I would be of the mindset that the most likely scenario is that the four of them are under house arrest."

"Frank, do you see these four coming home anytime soon?"

"Well, John, these negotiations were intended to reach an amicable solution for all parties involved. With the public attention to this case in both the U.S. and Canada, and both governments now having to deal with the new slant on this case, that is to say coming up with a solution that is not only amicable to both countries, but will also save face for both countries in the light they are viewed around the world, I would say this is going to be a long drawn out process."

"Thank you, Frank. I'm certain you will keep us informed with any further developments in this case."

"Yes, John. Our investigation is ongoing."

After the story aired, Susan just turned off the TV, and unhooked the phone. She had no intention of talking with anyone for the rest of the evening.

Chapter 24

Although Fran was once again becoming accustomed to the lifestyle she was living, even though she had never really considered Chartersville home, she was actually starting to feel homesick. Chartersville was now a working city again. Martial law had ended and normal law enforcement agencies were once again responsible for maintaining the peace. Most of the construction that had been destroyed as the result of the recent riots had now been replaced with new construction. Although, for the most part, things seemed to be operating as one would expect in Chartersville, there was still an aura of distrust among the residents of the city, especially when it came to any communication with law enforcement agencies.

Steven had an older brother that lived outside of Chartersville. The two didn't talk to each other a great deal of the time because both of their jobs took up a great deal of their time. It was not unusual for either of them to not immediately return each others calls, so Jerry was not really concerned when Steven had not returned his calls. Jerry's busy lifestyle kept him away from the current happenings in the world unless he made a specific effort to learn about them, so he wasn't really as abreast as he should be on what was going on in Chartersville. Thus, although one would think there wasn't a soul on Earth who was unaware of the Fruskin story, they would be wrong.

As time went on, however, and Jerry was continually unsuccessful at reaching Steven, he took it upon himself to stop by Steven and Fran's apartment the next time he was in Chartersville. Jerry was rather surprised to find the apartment vacant, and he visited the office to learn more. When he asked the property manager where the three had gone, the manager stated that company policy prohibited him from revealing any information.

Jerry answered the property manager with, "You are aware that there are steps that I can take that will allow me to eventually retrieve that information. I don't really have the time to do that, and I would venture to guess that you don't either."

The property manager answered with, "Let's take a walk."

The two walked the property and the property manager explained that the three were evicted for non-payment. The property manager had no contact with the three, so their belongings were temporarily placed in storage for later disposition. Jerry asked what would happen to their belongings. He was told that in order for the rightful owner to retrieve them, all back due rent and storage fees would have to be paid in full, or the property would eventually be auctioned off. When Jerry inquired how much that totaled, the property manager explained the total included one month's past due rent, a lease breaking fee that included one month's rent, and the property storage fees. When Jerry learned the amount, he just wrote a check for the amount owed, plus enough to keep Steven and Fran's property in storage for a while.

Jerry's next stop was Steven's workplace, where he learned that Steven had been gone for over two months, and he was no longer with the company. Jerry had began to sense that something was indeed very wrong and was determined to find out what was going on. He called information to find Susan Giddings number in an attempt to find out more but met with no success. The business he was in had forced him to keep abreast on some of the best cell phone directories, and he was able to locate Susan's number with one of those directories. When he learned from Susan what was going on, in no short order was he on his way to Drilton to learn more. Two and a half hours later, when Jerry met with Susan, Susan explained to him everything that had happened.

Susan was normally a strong person, but recent events had forced her to rethink what the right thing to do was. She shared the conversations that had taken place with Agent Benson with Jerry, including the agent's phone number. Jerry quickly contacted Agent Benson in an effort to find out more.

When Agent Benson answered the phone, and Jerry inquired about the whereabouts of Steven, Fran, Justin, and Joshua Fruskin, he responded, "I don't know how you got this number, but I can't comment on that case," and hung up the phone.

After Jerry hung up, he realized he needed to take some impromptu time off to sort this thing out. He contacted those he needed to in order to temporarily transfer his workload to those he could trust to continue the work he had started and who would keep him informed.

He now found himself on his way to Ruskville, a small town in southwestern Colorado, but it had an airport that provided connections to Denver, where Jerry planned to catch an international flight to Canada. Based on the information he had gathered from Susan, he flew directly to Ottawa from Canada. He had traveled internationally in the past, so a passport was not a concern.

Upon arriving in Ottawa, Jerry rented a car equipped with a GPS, and set out on a journey that he expected would lead him to his brother and his brother's family. After contacting the office of Canada's Minister of Public Safety, Jerry met with no success on obtaining any more information that might help him find his brother. Knowing that Steven, Fran, and Justin were in the custody of the Canadian Government, based on what Susan told him, Jerry rationalized that the three would probably be held in an isolated area. Not wanting to deal with government bureaucracy, on a hunch, Jerry contacted helicopter charter companies in the area to inquire about recent flights with three or more passengers to isolated areas. After repeatedly being told that passenger manifest were confidential, and even explaining that he didn't necessarily have to have the names of the passengers, just the origination, passenger count, and destination, Jerry still wasn't making any progress on the phone. He concluded that a personal visit to each of these charter companies might be in order.

After having no success with the first two, Jerry had limited success with the third. As he pulled into a gravel driveway that led to a very small building, he could see two helicopters to the left of the building and further back. Inside the tiny building was a counter toward the back and a door on each side of the building, each leading to the airfield. Behind the counter was a short, heavy set woman, in her late-forties with short hair, and as Jerry was about to find out, an attitude that certainly would cause him some hardship in finding out what he needed to know.

As Jerry approached the counter, the woman said, "May I help you?"

Jerry responded, "Yes, I need some information. I need to know if you have had any recent flights that included three passengers, a man and woman in their mid-forties and a sixteen-year-old."

"That's like asking me if it snows in March. Do you know how many passenger lists would fit that description?"

"My guess is that this flight would have been one-way and booked sometime in the last two months."

"Oh, well, my word, that narrows it down to at least half of them. Look, sir, even if I could narrow this down to the flight you're looking for, and I'm not saying that I could, I'm still not at liberty to divulge passenger manifest."

"What can you tell me?"

"I can tell you the date and time of departure, flight duration, arrival time, passenger count, and destination. That's it."

"Fine. Do you have a printed copy of that information available?"

"Cost you five bucks."

Jerry paid the woman the five bucks and obtained the list of flights for the past three months. Upon a review of this list, one of the flights caught his attention. It was a charter flight that had two legs. The first with no passenger count and a destination of Ottawa capital building. The second had a passenger count of three and a flight duration of 147 minutes. The thing that caught Jerry's eye the most, though, was the fact that this was the only flight on the list that did not list a destination.

Jerry had a lot of friends, and one of them was a helicopter pilot. A quick call to his friend revealed that a helicopter's average cruising speed was about 110 miles per hour. Some quick calculations revealed that a 147 minute flight would give an approximate radius of 270 miles, so he knew that he was facing a drive of less than five hours in any direction. Now he needed to narrow this down. That, as he was about to find out, was not going to be an easy task, but what he did for a living required perseverance in obtaining as much information as he could. The task at hand, he believed, was nothing more that what he already did on a daily basis.

A little research on his laptop revealed a list of licensed helicopter pilots in and around Ottawa and what companies they worked for. Once Jerry had that information, he was able to determine which pilots worked for the charter company he had obtained the list from. He had always been rather direct, and not wanting to speak with the woman that provided him with the list again, once again, with a little research, he was able to obtain phone numbers for the three pilots that worked for the company. He called all three of them and soon discovered that only one of them was working the day of the flight in question.

When he got a hold of the pilot that was working that day, they had a long conversation, as Jerry was intent on finding out what he needed to know in order to find his brother and his family.

Toward the end of the conversation, Jerry had finally made some progress as the pilot told him, "Look, I sympathize with your situation. I have a family myself. I'm certainly obliged to keep the destination of that flight confidential." The pilot continued with what Jerry considered an off-the-wall question, "Look, do you like seafood?"

Jerry asked, "Where did that come from?"

"Just answer the question. Do you like seafood."

"Not particularly."

"Just try this place, I'm sure you'll change your mind. I'm not quite sure of the directions, but if you have a GPS, I can give you the coordinates."

With that, Jerry knew he had struck gold, so he took the information from the pilot, plugged it into his GPS, and was now on his way to a destination that would bring him ever so close to his ultimate goal of finding Steven, Fran, and Justin. The drive took a little less than four hours and passed through some beautiful scenery and a lot of small towns.

Near the end of the drive, Jerry found himself in a heavily wooded area as his GPS simply stated, "Nearing destination."

This was slightly disconcerting because Jerry was in what he considered to be the absolute middle of nowhere. The only thing here was the road and thick woods. He passed a sign that said "Hidden Driveway" and pulled off here to better determine exactly where he was at.

As he did, his GPS stated, "Destination Arrival. Trip Complete."

Jerry found himself parked on a short gravel driveway that seemed to lead to nowhere. As he got out to look around, he discovered a short path that led to a clearing in the woods just large enough for a small helicopter to land. He knew he was close. He also knew that if the three of them were in the custody of the Canadian Government, as Susan had told him, in an isolated area like this, local law enforcement would have to be involved.

He got back in the car and determined that there was a small town just a short distance down the road. As he came into town, sure enough, there was a small seafood restaurant on the left side of the street. Jerry reassured himself that this was the helicopter pilot's out if any of this were to come to light.

As Jerry drove through town, on the right, at the end of this group of buildings that called itself a town, was a small building with one police car parked on the shoulder in front of it. Jerry parked behind the patrol car and went inside the station. It was just one room with two desks facing each other and a holding cell on the left. There was a heavy set man wearing a uniform, and a cowboy hat to match, sitting behind one of them.

As Jerry walked in the door, the man said, "What can I do you for, stranger?"

Jerry replied, "I'm looking for a place to stay for a couple of days."

"Only place I know is the Capitan place just outside of town, east of here, but I have it from a good source that place is occupied at the moment." The officer continued, "What brings you into town anyway?"

"I'm here to see if I can catch some fish."

Jerry started to leave as the officer said, "There ain't no lake 'round here."

Jerry replied, "You don't need a lake to fly fish," as he continued to walk out the door. He headed west out of town, and upon spotting a couple walking alongside the road, he pulled up alongside of them and asked if they knew where the Capitan place was.

The woman answered, "Oh yeah, I know that place well. Just keep heading down this road. Take the second left on Oasis, then you're going to take your third right. I can't remember the name of the street. No matter, it's the second driveway on the right. You can't miss it. It's a two-story, cedar-sided cabin, but I think that place is rented at the moment. I seen a car there yesterday."

Jerry followed the woman's directions and, sure enough, after he mad his way to the last street she told him to take, there stood the two-story, cedar-sided cabin where Steven, Fran, and Justin were, though he wasn't sure if Joshua was there.

Jerry knew that if his hunch was correct, and this was

where Steven, Fran, and Justin were because they were in the custody of the Canadian Government, he would have to be rather cautious in his attempt to confirm that his hunch was actually fact. With that in mind, Jerry set out to find a place to stay, but soon realized that what the officer told him earlier was absolutely correct. There certainly was no other place in town to stay, so he found himself driving a distance of another twenty miles just to find a place. He booked a room in the next small town he could use as kind of a base, but as things stood, he wouldn't be spending much time in that room.

In the next couple of days, Jerry spent his time keeping an eye on the cabin. It didn't take him long to realize that the only time someone would come out or go into the cabin was every twelve hours, 7:00 AM and 7:00 PM, in what Jerry now believed was a changing of the guards.

Jerry was one to react to what he saw, and he had every intention of confirming what he believed to be true. The third time he saw this ritual take place, he approached the man he saw coming out of the cabin just after the other had gone in.

Jerry asked the man, "Do you know who owns this cabin?"

The man answered, "Couldn't tell you for sure. We're renting from a leasing company."

"Can you tell me the name of the leasing company?"

"Why do you ask?" asked the man in reply to Jerry's question.

"I understand this is about the only rental cabin in town, and I'd be interested in renting when you leave."

"Well, one thing's for sure. You're absolutely right, this is the only rental cabin in town. But I'm afraid we have a long-term lease, so I don't see this cabin becoming available anytime in the near future. You'll have to find other accommodations."

Jerry pressed, "When does your lease expire?"

"I don't think that's any of your business. I just told you we have a long-term lease, and that means you're trespassing, so I suggest you get back in your vehicle and high-tail it out of here." With that, the man got into his car and drove away.

The man's reaction only served to strengthen Jerry's belief that this was the cabin where Steven, Fran, and Justin were. After the man left, Jerry left for a short time. He had every intention of returning to the cabin, however, he wanted to allow enough time for the man he talked with to get far enough away from the cabin before doing so. A couple of hours passed, and Jerry returned to the cabin. He walked up onto the covered porch and knocked on the door.

It took a couple of minutes, and a short man, in his mid-forties, wearing slacks and a polo shirt, answered the door, "May I help you?"

Jerry's profession had taught him to be very observant of everything that was going on around him, and as the man opened the door, although he didn't open it wide, Jerry was able to catch a short glimpse of Justin making his way through a doorway, now confirming everything Jerry had believed to be true.

Jerry knew he had to make plans to get Steven, Fran, and Justin out of there. He also knew that everything he said or did from this point forward would have a direct bearing on how he was going to accomplish that. Not wanting to give the man he was now talking to any indication of what his true purpose was, he kept his conversation with the man limited to what he had already discussed with the previous agent, and kept with the premise that he intended to rent the cabin for a fishing trip.

He answered the man's question, "I understand this cabin is about the only rental cabin in the area, and I was interested in renting it for a fishing trip. I was hoping you could tell me who you were renting it from?"

The man answered, "Well, this is a rental cabin, but I'm afraid we have a long-term lease with an option to renew. I'm afraid it's not going to be available any time soon."

Jerry pressed on, "Well, can you give me the name of the people you're renting it from?"

"Look, I just told you we had a long-term lease, so there's really no point in telling you that, is there?"

"How long is long-term?"

"Let me see if I can make this perfectly clear. We have no intention of giving up our lease any time soon, so I suggest you get back in that vehicle of yours and find other accommodations."

Jerry kept a close watch on the cabin over the next couple of days and eventually was able to seize an opportunity in a rare moment when Steven happened to be outside of the cabin. When Jerry saw Steven had strolled slightly into the woods at the back of the cabin, and could very well be out of sight of the agent inside, in what could almost be described as a quiet yell, Jerry was successfully able to get Steven's attention, though not exactly on the first try.

Now believing that he was isolated, Steven thought to himself that no one could possibly be there, and passed off Jerry's initial attempt as his mind playing tricks on him. When Jerry finally did get Steven's attention, Steven was as shocked as he possibly could be to see his brother standing there in the woods.

"What are you doing here?" asked Steven.

"Looking for you," replied Jerry. "Who else is with you?"

"Fran, Joshua, and Justin."

"Joshua's with you?" Jerry asked, slightly surprised and wanting to confirm what he heard.

"Yeah, Joshua's with us."

"Anyone else?"

"Agent Bryar."

"Yeah, I know. I talked to him."

Steven didn't reply to Jerry's last statement. It was nothing unusual for Jerry to ask a question he already knew the answer to. He thought to himself for a minute, "This has got to be where Joshua received this very trait from," as Joshua constantly made a habit of doing the very same thing. Nevertheless, Steven was very glad to see Jerry, as he was recently starting to question in his mind whether the four of them would ever get back to the United States. As things stood, Steven was about to find out that getting back to the U.S. was going to take a little while longer.

Chapter 25

Jerry told Steven, "We gotta get you guys out of there."

"Yeah, I think you're right," replied Steven. "They told us that they were working on getting us back to the United States, but it's been too long. How are we going to do that?"

"You tell me."

"Agent Bryar usually stays downstairs in the living room when we're asleep. The stairway downstairs actually leads to the kitchen, where the back door is. I think if I'm careful, after Agent Bryar thinks we're asleep, I could get us out the back door."

"When?"

"How about tonight?"

"That'll work," Jerry said in a confident manner while also implying that the rest was up to Steven.

"I'll meet you here tonight. Just watch for the lights upstairs to go out. We'll be down about ten minutes after that."

"I'll be here."

Steven went back into the cabin unaware of where Jerry went for the time being. At the first opportunity, when he was well out of earshot of Agent Bryar, he told Fran what the plans were.

Fran's reply to Steven was what he might expect, as she said, "Why can't we just stay here? They told us they're going to get us back to the U.S."

Steven said, "It's been too long, Fran. Something's wrong. I don't see us leaving anytime soon."

"I'm tired of running."

"Look, let's just go with Jerry, and we won't have to run

anymore."

"How can you be sure?"

"Trust me."

"That's what you said before, and look where it got us."

Nevertheless, Fran was Steven's wife, and over the years, for the most part, she had let Steven have the final say, especially when it came to major decisions, and this one could certainly be classified as a major decision. Although she had many apprehensions at this point, the biggest one was getting Justin downstairs and out the door without tipping off Agent Bryar.

Just before Steven retired for the evening, he was careful to leave the back door slightly open, in an effort not to alert Agent Bryar when the four of them left. When they were all upstairs, Fran told Joshua and Justin what their plans were. To prevent Justin from giving them away, an event that was all too common with Justin in the past when Fran tried to keep something a secret, she told Justin to walk down the stairs directly behind her and cover his mouth. As they made their way down the carpeted steps, as quietly as possible, Steven led the way with Fran directly behind him, Justin behind her, and Joshua in the back. When the four of them exited the cabin through the back door, Agent Bryar was in the living room, believing he had no reason to suspect anything was out of the ordinary. Joshua was careful not to shut the door all the way as he went through, thus ensuring that they could not be heard leaving the cabin.

When they had made their way through the woods at the back of the cabin, there stood Jerry where Steven had talked to him before.

As soon as Justin saw Jerry, he exclaimed, "Uncle Jerry!"

Jerry immediately replied, "Shh, your voice carries."

"What do you mean, 'carries'?" asked Justin.

"Don't talk. Someone might hear you."

"Who's going to hear me?"

Almost in unison, Steven, Fran, and Joshua said, "Don't

talk!" in an emphatic, yet whispered tone.

"So where do we go from here?" asked Steven to Jerry.

Jerry replied, "My car's right over there," as he motioned for the four of them to follow him.

When the five of them arrived at the car, Fran got in the front passenger's seat, while Steven, Joshua, and Justin got in the back. Jerry started the car and began driving down what appeared to be a short driveway.

Joshua commented, "Uncle Jerry, you don't have your lights on."

"I know. There's a reason for that," Jerry replied.

Satisfied with Uncle Jerry's answer, but still thinking, "This is dangerous," Joshua didn't say anything else, for quite a while for that matter. He had convinced himself, as he had done many times before, that he was right. When Jerry reached the roadway, he turned on his headlights.

After they had been on the road for a little while, Steven asked Jerry, "So where are we going?"

Jerry responded, "Look, I give it less than a couple of hours before that guy we left behind figures out we're gone. What do you figure's gonna happen then?"

"I suppose they'll be looking for us."

"I suppose you're right," Jerry answered in a calm, but rather snide answer.

They were soon to discover it was going to be less than a couple of hours. In no short order, Jerry and Fran could see flashers up ahead, in what appeared to be a roadblock. Jerry took a chance that they wouldn't see them, and turned off the road well ahead of the roadblock. After driving a short distance longer, he set his GPS to map an alternate route. Fran couldn't help but think to herself that now, once again, they were on the run.

Chapter 26

Meanwhile, somewhere near Canada's capital of Ottowa, negotiations continued with the U.S. and Canada in an effort to secure Steven, Fran, and Justin's release to the U.S. authorities. Once it was made known to the U.S. representatives involved in the negotiations that Canadian officials were well aware of the alleged crimes Steven, Fran, and Justin had committed in the United States, as Canada had been tracking the three prior to crossing the border, Canada's representatives for these negotiations seemed to set out on a new agenda that included attempting to rationalize justifiable behavior for each of the crimes the three allegedly committed.

Just as a representative of Canada's Department of Foreign Affairs was speaking, addressing a member of the U.S. Delegation, a man dressed in a blue suit walked through the double doors in the back of the room. Everyone in the room, including the man currently speaking was well aware that these meetings were closed, and anyone entering the room at this point would certainly be required to have the credentials to get past several security checkpoints.

In an effort to discount the interruption, the representative from Canada's Department of Foreign Affairs continued to speak, as the man who entered the room walked up to Jason Culver, Canada's Minister of Public Safety, and handed him a folded slip of paper. Jason was well aware that, at this point, all eyes were on him, but many years in public office had taught him to remain calm and professional in situations such as this. Knowing that the information he had just been provided with could only be of a sensitive matter, he read it in a manner that would draw the least amount of attention. That proved futile.

As soon as the representative from Canada's Department of Foreign Affairs took just a short pause to process his thoughts for his next statement, a representative from the U.S. Department of Justice, who seemed to be taking a lead with the U.S. delegation, began to speak, addressing Jason Culver, "Mr. Culver, do you have new information that is pertinent to this case?"

Well aware that both the U.S. and Canadian delegation already knew the answer to that question, it was imperative that Jason answer the question in a manner that would meet the expectations of the highest levels of the Canadian Government, for whatever he said next would directly affect how these negotiations would proceed, and how Canada was about to be portrayed in a world light.

In an unexpected move that would prove detrimental to his career, yet feeling a moral obligation to proceed, Jason answered, "I'm afraid I do."

"Would you care to enlighten us?"

"Gentlemen, it appears that at approximately 0200 hours this morning, an agent with Canada's national and federal intelligence services, who was on a special assignment to conduct protective services for Steven, Fran, Justin, and Joshua Fruskin, discovered that the four of them were no longer under Canadian protective custody."

"Mr. Culver, would you care to break down your previous statement into further detail. Perhaps, enlightening us with information that would allow us to determine whether the three these negotiations are centering around are still in a position that would give purpose to continuing these negotiations, and for that matter, why Joshua Fruskin was under Canadian protective custody?"

"Gentlemen, at this point, Steven, Fran, Joshua, and Justin Fruskin are not in the custody of any Canadian agency. Joshua Fruskin was placed in the protective custody of the Canadian Government when he was exposed to information that could compromise these very negotiations."

"Well now, Mr. Culver, isn't that just a fresh new pile of dog doo-doo that we're now all obligated to clean up?"

At that point, a spokesman from the U.S. Delegation with the Federal Bureau of Investigating began to speak, "Gentlemen, in light of these new developments, I propose that the U.S. law enforcement agencies that are currently involved in this case have an opportunity to work directly with Canadian law enforcement in the apprehension of these four."

Mr. Culver responded, "Gentlemen, I am certain that my department and those agencies under my jurisdiction are perfectly capable of, as your government has so elegantly put it, 'cleaning up this pile of dog doo-doo' on our own. Of course, we will continue to cooperate as we have done in the past in the sharing of information deemed necessary to achieve a successful result to this investigation."

The representative from the U.S. Department of Justice replied, "Mr. Culver, I believe that I speak for the entire U.S. Delegation when I say that your government's definition of a successful result of this investigation is not one that the U.S. shares. Nevertheless, I am inclined to agree with the FBI when it comes to the need for a joint U.S./Canadian law enforcement investigation of this case, and I'm talking about one that would include much more than the sharing of information."

Mr. Culver responded, "Gentleman, although I stand by my previous statement, I am a party to saying that I, as well as my government, recognize the benefits a joint investigation can provide regarding this case. At the same time, I am well aware of the not-so-desirable consequences a joint investigation could result in. With that in mind, I propose that we recess these negotiations until an opportunity has been provided to cascade the information gained at this session to those in both of our governments who's jurisdiction might fall into making a final decision in how we intend to proceed on matters that have been discussed."

The U.S. Department of Justice responded, "I'm inclined to agree with you. As far as the U.S. Delegation is concerned, these proceedings are in recess. In accordance with procedures established previously, all of you will be notified of exactly when these proceedings will reconvene."

At that point, Mr. Culver stated, "I concur. At this time the Canadian Delegation is in recess with regards to these proceedings. All of you will be notified as to when these proceedings will reconvene."

With that, at least for the time being, it appeared that Steven, Fran, Joshua, and Justin's fate might now be in the hands of both the U.S. and Canadian Governments, who had very different agendas on how this investigation was to end.

Chapter 27

Jerry, Steven, Fran, Joshua, and Justin now found themselves somewhere in southwestern Manitoba. Their intention was to cross the border into the U.S. in an isolated area, much in the same manner they had originally crossed the border into Canada. However, as they were about to find out, things had heated up much more than they expected, and crossing the border might be a lot harder than they had expected.

Jerry was well aware that the Canadian police would have every border crossing, no matter how small, staffed with the mounties necessary to apprehend all of them. His plans were to find an area of the border where Steven, Fran, Justin, and Joshua could cross on their own on foot without drawing attention to themselves, while he intended to return the car to a branch of the rental agency and fly back to the U.S. As they traveled through the back roads of southwestern Manitoba, near the U.S. border with North Dakota, they discovered a river east of a small border crossing that they believed would be ideal for the four of them to cross on foot. Jerry managed to get the vehicle down a small dirt road where, for the time being, it would be well hid. He had every intention of making sure the four of them made it across the border into the U.S. safely.

After about a quarter-mile hike down the banks of the river, only expecting to see a sign denoting the U.S./Canadian international boundary, what they saw next would prove only that they would be forced to make a change in plans. Up ahead, along the banks of the river, was a small camp with two men in uniform, one a Canadian Border Patrol agent, the other a U.S.

Border Patrol agent.

The five of them turned around, and Jerry looked at Steven and asked, "Anything else you want to tell me?" in a tone indicating that Steven had not been comprehensive when doling out information to Jerry.

Indeed, Steven had failed to pass on bits and pieces of information about their journey to Jerry, mostly about the parts that involved what the U.S. considered crimes, and he knew Jerry would, too, even if Steven felt they were justified.

Knowing that Jerry probably already knew the answer to the question he just asked, Steven cautiously answered, "Not really."

This was of no avail, as Jerry's means of providing himself a living involved investigating matters where the persons directly involved were reluctant to provide him with all of the information he needed, and Jerry's thought process always included a line of questions that seemed to satisfy his quest for information.

"Can any of you think of any reason both the U.S. and Canadian law enforcement agencies might be looking for you, aside from what you've already told me?"

Justin was the first to volunteer, "Well, we kinda stole a car, two of them, actually."

Steven then added, "It seems we were forced to make some decisions some people might consider crimes."

Jerry asked, "So, would that be in Canada, the U.S., or both?"

Steven replied, "No, not in Canada. Just the U.S."

"Just?" Jerry asked in a voice indicative of a thought that Steven's answer held no responsibility for what the three had done. "What all did you do?"

"Well, there was the cars, trespassing, maybe breaking and entering, probably something that might be called unauthorized transportation on a privately owned train, and we sorta borrowed a police car."

"What would possess you to do those things?"

"Well, we really didn't have a choice."

"You always have a choice," replied Jerry with a tone expected of a big brother intending to teach you something. Jerry continued, "Never mind, what's done is done. We can't change the past. Now we just have to fix this." At this point, Jerry was rationalizing to himself that the four of them, at least Steven, Fran, and Justin, might be better off staying in Canada. "You guys should have told me this before. You guys can't cross the border, at least the three of you anyway."

Joshua said, "I wanna stay with Mom and Dad," in a voice that indicated certainty, and if history was any indication of future, he had no intention of doing otherwise.

Jerry replied, "OK, let's think about this. What's the best way to get you guys back to the U.S.? You know, Steven, you guys might be better off in Canada."

"We're going back to the United States," replied Steven. "What if we tried to cross somewhere in Alaska first, and then figured out how to get back home?"

"That's not a bad idea. There is a whole bunch of wilderness up there, especially if we go through the Yukon. Practically no chance of getting caught, except maybe by bears."

"Bears?" asked Justin in reply to Jerry, indicating his apprehension.

"You don't worry about the bears, Justin, for now, anyway," Jerry answered in hopes of relieving Justin's fears for now.

Jerry now revised his plans to including getting these four all the way across Canada to the Alaskan border in the Yukon and across the border to the U.S. He also knew he wasn't going to be back in the U.S. anytime in the very near future. So the five of them returned to the car, and Jerry made the necessary arrangements with the rental car agency to keep the car for a few more days.

When Jerry mapped his route to the little town in Alaska, where he believed it might be possible for the four to cross the border relatively unnoticed, he discovered that this trip consisted of forty-nine hours of driving time, slightly more than that in reality. He knew there would be times he would have to deviate from this route in order to avoid what might be the inevitable if they did not. However, he and Steven both believed that the Canadian authorities would be thinking that the four they were looking for would attempt to cross the border somewhere over the lower forty-eight, and that's where they would be concentrating their efforts to find them. Fortunately for the five of them, their hunch would prove to be true.

As the five of them began their long drive across the beautiful country of Canada, at first Jerry and Steven took turns driving. Eventually, they were able to convince Fran to share in this monumental undertaking. The fact that neither Steven nor Fran were listed as drivers on the rental car agreement didn't seem to bother Jerry. Perhaps he had some inside information that due to some technicality, it was actually okay for the two of them to be driving, or maybe, just maybe, Jerry had actually resigned himself to the fact that based on the circumstances at hand, such a small indiscretion would not be the end of the world.

As the five of them crossed this country, they saw very little law enforcement, at least, any that might appear to be looking for them. Provincial route after provincial route, even the longer stints of driving on Canada's major highways proved to be uneventful. However, their luck was about to run out, at least for the five of them, it would appear that way.

Shortly after crossing into the Yukon territory from British Columbia, Jerry's rear-view mirror lit up the familiar flashers that one would recognize in any country. Jerry pulled off to the right shoulder, expecting the police unit to go around him. He had no such luck. Jerry slowly brought the car to a stop. The Mountie stopped behind him with his vehicle slightly to the left of Jerry's. He walked up to the driver's side window, that Jerry had already rolled down in anticipation of the Mountie standing next to it.

The Mountie then said those all-so-familiar words most all of us have heard as the first line of questioning from law enforcement, no matter what country you might be in, "May I see your driver's license, registration, and proof of financial responsibility, please?"

Jerry handed the Mountie his driver's license, along with the paper work the rental car agency had instructed him to give law enforcement in the event of just such the present circumstances. When the Mountie saw that Jerry possessed a U.S. driver's license, he asked to see his passport in addition to the paperwork Jerry had already provided him. The tension and silence from Steven, Fran, Justin, and Joshua was noticeably thick, and the Mountie picked up on it, but apparently felt he had no other indication that any of them had done anything outside the current scope of Canadian law. He just continued his intended line of questioning, although with a much closer examination of the details in Jerry's response to them.

"Do you know why I stopped you?" the Mountie asked.

Jerry responded that he did not, and the Mountie explained, "The speed limit on this particular provincial route is 85 KPH and you were doing upwards of 100 KPH"

Jerry expected the Mountie to walk back to his patrol car for the usual interim wait while the Mountie looked up the information he had on his computer. Much to Jerry's amazement, he did not.

He simply said, "Mr. Fruskin, when you're in Canada, and especially the Yukon territories, we expect you to abide by our laws, just as we would expect from our Canadian citizens. Just slow down, and enjoy your visit to Canada." With that the Mountie walked back to his patrol car and waited for Jerry to leave.

As they pulled back onto the road, and the patrol car disappeared from sight in the distance, all five of them breathed a much needed sigh of relief. It took a little while, but the comfort levels of the five eventually returned to normal, and their conversations were only centered around how close they all felt that was for just a short time, until all five of them realized it would be much better to talk about something else.

Many hours later, they reached the Alaskan border, only

because Steven and Jerry had both agreed that it would be better for them to go well up into the Yukon territory. Both of them believed it would be much easier to cross the border into Alaska further up into the Yukon. As it turned out, they would be right. As they came within miles of the border, Jerry turned down a dirt road that headed south.

According to the map that was in their possession, there was a river south of the road they had been on, and both Jerry and Steven thought attempting to follow the riverbed to cross into the U.S. might prove to be successful this time. As the miles passed, the narrow little dirt road began to get rougher with each passing mile. The five of them persevered and, eventually, the road led them to a narrow river. Jerry and Steven looked at the map carefully and determined they would have to follow the river upstream to cross into the United States. Although secretly, Jerry may have wanted to drop the four off and wish them good luck, that wasn't in his nature, and he intended to fulfill what he felt was his obligation to see the four of them across the border and into the U.S.

So began the long hike upstream in the cold weather, although not so cold it proved to be unbearable for any of them. What seemed like hours of hiking would eventually lead them to what someone might think of as a joke, but, for them, was a welcome sight. Someone had simply nailed two hand-painted metal signs to a tree that simply read, "Leaving Canada" on the side they were approaching and "Leaving United States" on the other side of the tree. Although Jerry was extremely happy to see the four of them had made it back to the U.S., he was still apprehensive, as he knew for Steven, Fran, Joshua, and Justin, their journey was far from over.

Jerry's intention was to return the rental car to the nearest agency and fly back to the U.S., so, for now, all of them would have to say their goodbyes. After some very lengthy goodbyes, and other conversation, Jerry finally left, and the four continued to make their way upriver until Steven felt he was well into the U.S. As dusk began to fall, the temperature began to drop, and Steven was very worried as to what they would do for shelter for the evening.

As they hiked a little further, Fran yelled, "Those are boats!"

"What are you talking about?" asked Steven.

"Look, up the river. Those are boats."

Steven looked up the river, and he did see something, though, at the moment, it was unrecognizable to him. As the four stood there for a moment, Steven could tell as the objects grew closer, these were indeed boats. Well, to be more precise, canoes, actually, and there was a group of four of them, with two people in each.

As the canoes approached the area where Steven, Fran, Justin, and Joshua were standing, the people on them could see that the four of them were shivering in the cold, and the gentlemen in the canoe closest to them yelled, "Do you guys need any help?"

Fran was the first to yell, "Yes, we do!" and all four canoes banked on the rocky shore next to them.

The one that initially asked if they needed help continued, "What are you guys doing out here?"

Steven answered, "We're lost," rationalizing to himself his answer was within the confines of the truth because he truly did not know where they were except for the fact that they were finally in the United States.

The man answered, "Well, you're a long way from civilization. You can camp with us tonight, if you like. We each brought our own tents, so we could have a little room, but under the circumstances, four of us can double up and let you four use the other two tents. Sleeping bags are going to be another issue though. We only have a couple of extras, so you guys will have to use them as a blanket in each tent. They're good for up to negative fifty-five degrees, so you should be relatively comfortable."

After some conversation with all eight of them, Steven and Fran learned that the eight of them were part of a church group that was on a prearranged outing for a river trip that would take them across the Canadian border. They had already made arrangements with the Canadian Government to cross the border into Canada. The eight of them had been very careful to make sure that they were all meticulous in packing the provisions that they needed for the trip. As a result, Steven, Fran, Joshua, and Justin had the luxury of eating a hot dinner cooked over a campfire that evening. After some lengthy conversations with the eight, the evening came to a close and Steven, Fran, Joshua, and Justin turned in for the evening. Joshua and Justin took one tent, and Steven and Fran took the other. After climbing into the tent with Steven, Fran thought it a miracle that at the beginning of what would be a very treacherous journey through the Alaskan wilderness, they now had shelter from the weather, food in their stomach, and a warm sleeping bag they could use as a blanket.

After the two of them had curled up under the open sleeping bag, Fran looked at Steven and said, "Someone must be watching over us."

Steven simply replied, "He is," and the two of them went to sleep for the evening.

Morning came, and Steven and Fran woke to the smell of something cooking over an open campfire. It turned out the eight had awoken much earlier than Steven and Fran, and had some luck with regards to catching some fish. The two dined on a breakfast of fish and granola bars, as did Joshua and Justin, who woke up shortly after their parents did.

After some discussion on what would be the best way to get the four of them out of their, all of them agreed it would be best to have a member of their congregation take the four to civilization while the rest continued their journey. One of the eight who had been on this trip before told Steven they would take the four of them downriver a short distance to a service road where they should wait to be picked up.

"We didn't see any service road," Fran said in reply to the man's statement.

The gentleman just replied, "Trust me. It's there."

After breaking camp and loading all the gear into the canoes, Steven, Fran, Joshua, and Justin each took a seat in the middle of four separate canoes, and they continued down river for a short time until they reached a section that had somewhat of a marshy bank on the right side of the shore. This is where they banked along the shore.

The man they had been talking to before explained there was a path that led up to a dirt turn-around where they should wait to be picked up. He even provided the four of them with some jerky and granola bars they could snack on while they waited.

They waited for about two hours and, eventually, a white van arrived and pulled to the side of the small area at the end of the road that had been described to them by their recently acquired friends as a turn-around. A thin man with long hair, a mustache, and beard got out of the van from the driver's seat. He couldn't have been much older then his mid-twenties, and he was wearing blue jeans and a checkered flannel shirt.

As he walked toward them he said, "You must be the four Dave was telling me about. So how did you guys end up way out here?"

"Long story," Steven replied.

"Well, let's get you four aboard my bus," with a tone of voice one might construe as filled with kindness and somehow indicated he was just here to help and he was not going to pry any further.

Steven thought it strange that the man would call the van a bus, but when the four of them boarded the van from the passenger's side, there was an aisle with seats designed for two in a row next to the aisle. The van was rather lengthy and appeared it could seat twelve in addition to the driver. The road they were on was a rough dirt road that was filled with its share of ruts. It eventually led them to another dirt road that they turned south on. The man driving was very friendly and did his best to make conversation with the four, although it seemed he was being careful not to ask too many questions with reference to their circumstances in what seemed to be a purposeful effort not to pry. It seemed one would expect this dirt road to eventually begin a stretch where they would find themselves traveling on a paved road. They had no such luck. The road continued its dirt makeup for many miles to come, although this one seemed to have less ruts in it.

Eventually, the five of them arrived at a crossroads with another dirt road. Along the road there were a few small buildings. There was a small store that also served as a bank. In front of the store was a dirt and gravel parking lot with one gas pump near the front of the lot next to the road. Next to the store was a tiny log building with gold colored letters near the top that read, "U.S. Post Office, Stewart, Alaska". Across the street was a building that had two garage doors on one side of it and a hand-painted sign that looked like someone had made at home above the main part of the building that read, "Stewart Hardware and Automotive Repair". The remainder of the buildings along the road, and there weren't very many, were all rather small houses, most of them built in a fashion that would make one wonder whether a building code existed, or at least if there were anyone enforcing it. Steven and Fran both thought to themselves that this has got to be the smallest town they had ever seen.

They pulled up next to the pump in the store's parking lot, and the man driving said, "I'll be right back up. You're welcome to come in if you like," and he got out of the driver's seat and headed across the parking lot into the store.

Steven and Fran did not take the man up on his offer, though Joshua and Justin wanted to. Steven didn't think it was a good idea for the two to go in, but Fran told Steven he was being overprotective and to let Justin and Joshua go into the store. He reluctantly agreed and told Fran that they had to be careful. They didn't know who all was looking for them at this point.

Fran replied to Steven's statement, "They're not looking for us in Alaska. They think we're still somewhere in Canada or somewhere near the border down there."

"How do you know that?" replied Steven.

"I just do."

Shortly thereafter, the man returned to the van and pumped the gas he had just purchased, while Joshua and Justin got back inside the van.

Joshua and Justin each had a candy bar in their hands and Fran asked, "Where did you get those?"

Fran knew the answer to her own question and this was her way of asking how they paid for them.

Joshua just looked down, seemingly apprehensive to answer the question, while Justin blurted out, "Eric bought them for us."

It was at that moment that both Steven and Fran realized, in all this time, they somehow had not made an effort to learn the name of the man that drove them into civilization from the middle of nowhere. After Eric finished pumping the gas he purchased, he got back into the van, and he started the engine back up.

He said, "Our church is just down the street at the edge of town. That's where we're headed."

When the five of them arrived at the church, Eric said, "Come on inside. There is someone I'd like you to meet," and he got out of the van first.

Sensing Steven's apprehension, Fran said, "You gotta cut this out. It'll be fine," in a reassuring voice.

Fran was well aware, however, of Steven's tendency for worry, as they had been married over twenty-one years, and if there was anything she had learned in that time, telling Steven not to worry was somewhat like telling a rock not to be hard. Even if he did hear her, he had no intention to, or simply couldn't, change his behavior, although Fran thought "wouldn't" might be a better choice to describe it.

When they walked into the tiny church, there was a room that was designed to be a foyer before entering the auditorium, much like any church. To the right of them were a men's and women's restroom, and on the left was the entrance to the auditorium. Eric led them into the auditorium, and a short, professional looking man, wearing khaki's and a polo shirt, met them near the front of the auditorium. The man introduced himself as Shaugn Trevers and said he was the pastor of the church.

He continued, "I understand you four have had quite a journey. I'd like to learn more about it, if I could."

Steven just looked at Fran with an expression that would imply he was seeking her approval. Fran only returned another look that was all to familiar for Steven and obviously indicated that she felt this was Steven's decision to make. This way of communicating was something that developed during their marriage, and had been refined over the years, almost to an art form. Steven resigned himself to the fact that he had to trust somebody, and he certainly needed some guidance as to what to do next. He reasoned to himself, who better than a pastor to do that.

He answered the pastor's request, "Is there somewhere we can talk?"

The pastor replied, "Sure, my office is right through here," motioning to the door on the left side of the stage.

He somehow made room in the tiny office for all of them, digging up a couple of chairs from a room next door. After sitting down, both Steven and Fran revealed their story to the pastor, sparing no detail that either of them felt necessary to indicate the reasons why they did all the things they did during the course of their long journey. The pastor listened with keen interest, and during the course of the conversation, he asked the questions he felt he needed to, in what Steven felt was a line of questioning that was designed to help the pastor understand and possibly justify Steven, Fran, and Justin's actions.

After a very lengthy conversation with the four, the pastor reasoned to himself that in God's eyes, Steven, Fran, and Justin's actions were justified, albeit, not all of them. Nevertheless, he felt himself and his congregation seemed to be obligated to the four, so he offered to allow the four of them to stay in a room that had a small kitchenette set up in it that the congregation typically used for fellowship from time to time. Steven accepted the pastor's offer and was somewhat relieved that the four had a place to stay for the time being.

Later that week, during Sunday services, the pastor told the congregation about their newly acquired guests and asked the congregation to give in a special collection that was intended to help the four continue their journey. The congregation was successful in raising enough money to buy the four a one-way bus ticket to the western coast of southeast Alaska, where Steven and Fran planned to somehow make their way back into the United States from there. Steven wasn't exactly sure how he was going to do that, as he specifically wanted to avoid entering Canada again, knowing that, under the circumstances, it would be virtually impossible for the four of them to enter the United States again.

Later that week, the pastor presented Steven with a one-way bus ticket for each of them to Sitka, Alaska, a small town on the western coast of southeast Alaska, although it would be considered a large city in comparison to the town they were in now. Sitka was also a port of call for several cruise lines.

The pastor handed Steven an additional envelope and said, "The congregation was able to raise a little money in addition to the bus ticket for whatever else you might need."

Steven thought it would be rude to look in the envelope, and instead, chose to stick the envelope in his pocket.

The pastor said, "Come on. I'll drive you to the bus station."

It turned out that the bus station was the same store they had stopped at when they had originally came into town, and when they arrived, the bus was already in the parking lot waiting for them.

Just before the four boarded the bus, the pastor told them, "God be with you on this journey. Our thoughts and prayers are with you. I know in my heart that everything is going to work out for the four of you."

The four of them boarded the bus. The bus was relatively empty. There were only three other passengers on the bus at the moment. The four of them boarded and took a seat toward the back. Joshua and Justin sat next to each other behind their parents. Steven was worried that they would have to pass through Canada to reach Sitka. When he asked the driver exactly what route they would take in order to reach their destination, the driver explained that they would be utilizing the Alaskan Marine Highway.

When Steven asked the driver what the Alaskan Marine Highway was, the driver asked Steven, "You folks aren't from around here, are you? The Alaskan Marine Highway is a ferry system. The one we're going to use is a boat that will take us along the southeast coast of Alaska. Some beautiful scenery there. You won't be disappointed."

The driver just assumed the four were on a family vacation, and as far as Steven was concerned, that was fine with him. The long journey toward Alaska's southeastern coast found Justin sleeping most of the way. He wasn't much for scenery and would much rather spend his time sleeping, since he had no video game to play. Somehow, Joshua had managed to keep his laptop with him the entire time. He had been careful to use it only when necessarily as of recent. It was amazing the laptop still held a charge, so Joshua was content to work on his computer. Fran would rather have had a book in her hand, but because she did not, she was forced to listen to Steven rant and rave about how beautiful the scenery was, all the while pretending to be just as excited.

Earlier, Steven had an opportunity to look in the envelope the pastor had given him and discovered there was just a little over five hundred dollars in it. He was grateful for the money and knew it would come in very handy for incidentals, however, at the moment, he had no idea how the four of them were going to get back to the lower forty-eight. Hours went by, and after a short stop in a small town for lunch and refreshments, the bus continued its journey to the coastal town of Valdez.

After arriving in Valdez, the bus pulled into a parking lot next to the blue waters of what appeared to be a rather large bay. The driver then made an announcement over the loudspeaker that there would be about a forty-five minute wait for the ferry.

Justin obviously didn't hear it because it didn't take long at all for him to ask, "Why did we stop?"

Fran answered, "We're waiting for the ferry."

Justin replied, "What's a ferry?"

Fran explained to Justin that a ferry transported vehicles across water to a land destination. The driver had not made an announcement that it was alright to leave the bus, however, upon parking, he had opened the door and he, along with some passengers, disembarked. Joshua asked Fran if he could get out and see the ocean.

Once again, Steven was apprehensive and was the first to respond, "I don't think that's a real good idea."

Fran looked at Steven and said, "Stop it."

She then answered Joshua, "Yes, you can get out and see the ocean."

Joshua started to get up with computer in hand, and Fran looked at Joshua and said, "Leave your computer here."

Steven was obviously upset with Fran's response, as he perceived it as insubordination. Fran could feel Steven's dissatisfaction with her actions and believed that she was now in for the silent treatment. In a predictable fashion, Steven got out of his seat and went with both Joshua and Justin, all the while not saying a word. Fran hated it when Steven was like this, and she had no intention of accompanying the three of them off the bus. In a move that Fran considered an act of sheer kindness, one of the passenger's offered Fran a book to read. It wasn't one of her usual authors, but she was more than grateful to have it.

Although Steven was still upset with Fran, the ocean seemed to have a calming effect, and it wasn't long before Steven's anger subsided. Although both Joshua and Justin wanted to get their feet wet in the water at the edge of the ocean, Steven was careful to keep them a safe distance, especially since Justin couldn't swim. Steven knew had Fran been with them, the two of them would most certainly be arguing about whether or not to let the boys get close to the water. So for now, both Joshua and Justin were content to venture along the beach a safe distance away. Joshua was more interested in the shells that he found, while Justin seemed to be most interested in just exactly what he could make out of the sand.

The time went by relatively fast, and eventually a boat appeared over the horizon. As the boat got closer, the few passengers that had disembarked from the bus began to return to it, as well as the driver, prompting Steven, Joshua, and Justin to do the same. The ferry eventually arrived at a dock near the shoreline, and there seemed to be a type of bridge that allowed vehicles to access the ferry from the road.

Once everyone had boarded the bus again, the driver was very careful to make sure all of his passengers were accounted for. Over the loudspeaker, the driver carefully explained that upon boarding the ferry, passengers on the bus would be required to disembark from the bus and would not have any access to their personal belongings until the ferry reached its destination, so it was important for passengers to make sure they had in their possession everything they felt necessary to have for the remainder of the trip. Both Joshua and Justin thought it strange that people could drive their vehicles over a bridge and right onto the boat. Once the bus had boarded the boat, a crew member in the parking area guided the driver to the space specially designated for the bus, where it would remain for the remainder of the trip.

Once the bus had came to a stop and was parked, the driver's voice could once again be heard over the loudspeaker, "Ladies and gentlemen, all passengers are required to disembark at this point. You will have an opportunity to retrieve the items you deem necessary for the remainder of the trip. You will not have access to the bus again until we reach our final destination. We will be aboard the ferry for approximately sixteen hours. For those of you who purchased a stateroom as part of your trip, your cabin information can be found on your ticket. You will need to present this information to the appropriate crew member to receive access to your cabin. If you did not purchase a cabin, there are appropriate sleeping areas in designated sections aboard the boat. All passengers will have access to food and beverage services, which range from vending machines to a full restaurant. Sitka is also the final destination for this ferry. With that in mind, you will be notified when it is appropriate to return to the bus. Please enjoy this portion of your trip. The views from the Alaskan Marine Highway are nothing short of spectacular."

When the driver had finished with his announcement, he disembarked from the bus and opened the luggage compartment to retrieve passenger's belongings. As Steven and Fran retrieved the two duffel bags containing what basically consisted of about three changes of clothes for each of the four of them, both of their thoughts returned to the congregation in the tiny town of Stewart and the kindness provided by them, even providing the much needed clothing that was now in their possession. The boys were anxious to go up to the deck; however, Fran told both of them to wait for a minute and not to go anywhere without their parents. Joshua and Justin both recognized the tone of her voice as being adamant in what she was saying. It was a rare occasion when Fran used that tone, and Joshua and Justin had no intention of questioning her when she did, at least not out loud, anyway.

Once Steven and Fran had gotten themselves organized, the four of them headed up to the deck. After some time had passed, the boat eventually pulled away from the docking area. It was interesting to watch as the docks disappeared in the distance. Already, the views from the boat were nothing short of spectacular. Fran was never really enthralled with such beauty, although she often pretended to be for Steven's benefit. It seemed the boys could care less either way. It didn't take long, however, for Fran to tell Steven that she was hungry. Very conscious of the fact that they still had a long trip ahead of them, and not knowing exactly where their journey would take them, Steven was predictably cautious on how he replied to Fran's statement.

"We can get something from the vending machines," replied Steven.

Fran's reply was equally predictable, and although she had never been high-maintenance, far from it, in fact, there were times she just wanted what she wanted, and this was one of those times.

"I don't want something from the vending machines. I want to eat in the restaurant."

"You don't even know what's in the vending machines," replied Steven in an attempt to get her to see things his way. He would, however, if history was any indication, be unsuccessful in trying to get her to see things in what he felt was a logical point of view.

"I don't care. I want real food," Fran replied adamantly.

Steven reluctantly agreed, only because he would rather give in to her request than have to deal with a pouty attitude from Fran for the remainder of the ferry trip.

When the four of them sat down at the table at the restaurant, Fran ordered what she thought was a much needed cola, while Justin ordered root beer. Both Steven and Joshua ordered water, though both had their own reasons for doing so. Joshua thought water was the healthier option. Steven was thinking about how he could stretch the finances they now had as far as possible. When Fran looked at the menu, she was very happy to see one of her favorite dishes under the seafood section.

Fran exclaimed, "They have Alaskan snow crab!"

This was where Steven couldn't help but to put his foot down, "You're not ordering snow crab. We can't afford it," and he was quick to point out the portion of the menu that contained sandwiches.

Fran settled on a hamburger and fries, while the rest of them had cheeseburgers and fries. After eating, the four of them found a group of comfortable lounge chairs in a covered solarium. Fran leaned back in her chair and continued to read the book she was given on the bus, while Joshua worked on his laptop. Steven and Justin found themselves exploring the boat. After a couple of hours, they returned to the solarium. Eventually, night fell and the four of them found themselves falling asleep in what turned out to be rather comfortable lounge chairs.

The next morning, all four of them woke up rather early. This time, Steven was successful in convincing Fran that vending machines were the best option for breakfast. Fran settled on a banana nut muffin and some apple juice, while Steven had coffee and a breakfast bar. The boys also had breakfast bars and juice, although it took some convincing from Joshua for Justin to decide on a breakfast bar, as Justin thought an apple pie would be a much better option.

For Fran and Joshua, the day started out as a repeat of the previous night, as far as activities were concerned. Steven and Justin decided to explore the boat once again, while Fran and Joshua stayed in the solarium. A short while later, Steven and Justin returned to the solarium to tell Fran and Joshua that they discovered the boat had a small theater. It seemed the next showing was in fifteen minutes, and although Fran wasn't interested, both Steven and Justin managed to convince Joshua to go with them. When the three sat down in the theater, they initially had most of the auditorium to themselves, but just before the film started, the theater began to fill up, with only a few seats remaining empty. The film was on Alaskan's southeastern coast, the very route they were traveling. It offered spectacular views of the coastline, a history of towns along the route, as well as places to explore and activities offered in the towns. It was a short film, although rather informative, and Steven thought to himself that if things ever returned normal, he would like to come back here someday.

The day passed and eventually the ferry reached its destination. As Steven and Joshua stood on the deck next to the railing, they both could see the dock in the distance. They returned to the solarium only to find Fran and Justin still in the lounge chairs, and Fran still making good use of the book she was reading. With some convincing, Steven was able to get Fran to put away her book and head toward the area where the bus had been parked for the duration of the journey. Fran felt they had plenty of time, as there had been no announcement made yet, and she felt the further need to make her point by telling Steven to quit his worrying, as the bus was not going to leave without them.

Just as Fran was through telling Steven not to worry, an announcement could be heard over the ship's loudspeaker, "Ladies and gentlemen, we will be docking in Sitka in approximately ten to fifteen minutes. At this time we would like to ask all passengers to prepare for disembarking, as Sitka is the final destination for this particular ferry. If you have further travel plans, please refer to the itinerary that was provided at the time of your ticket purchase. Access to vehicle storage areas will be available once the ship has docked. Thank you for traveling the Alaskan Marine Highway, and please enjoy the remainder of your journey."

"See, I told you. We have plenty of time," Fran told Steven with the sole purpose of reinforcing the fact that she was right.

Shortly thereafter, the boat docked. Steven, Fran, Joshua, and Justin made their way back to the area where the bus had been parked. The four of them, along with the other passengers, boarded the bus again for the short trip to Sitka's bus station.

On the way to the station, Fran asked Steven, "So, where do we go from here?"

She was hoping for a well-planned answer, however, Steven's response would not meet with expectations.

"I haven't planned that far, yet," replied Steven.

Fran's silence in response to Steven's answer was an obvious indication of her displeasure with the answer. When the bus arrived at the station, the four collected their belongings and headed for the inside of the bus station, not knowing what they were going to do next.

As they entered the bus station, they could hear the remainder of an announcement over the station's loudspeaker, "...with connections to Alaskan Cruise Lines for ports of call in Vancouver, Seattle, Los Angeles, and San Diego."

Steven looked at Fran and said, "I have an idea."

"What?" replied Fran.

"Just wait here."

"Where are you going?" Fran asked as Steven headed toward the station's front desk.

A short while later, Steven returned and said to Fran, "We're getting back on the bus."

"What do you mean 'We're getting back on the bus'?" Fran asked, wondering what Steven was up to.

"We're getting back on the bus. We're going back to the docks."

"Why?"

"I'll explain later. Let's go."

"But we don't have any tickets," Fran said, intending to ask the question of how they were going to board the bus without paying for the ride.

"We don't need any. The man at the counter said it would be alright."

Fran didn't know what Steven was planning, however, years of marriage had taught here that there were times when she just had to trust him. Fran felt this was on of those times.

As the bus returned to the docks, there was a large cruise ship docked. On the bow of the massive ship were the words "Alaskan Cruise Lines".

As the bus pulled into a parking lot next to the docks, the driver made an announcement, "Passengers ticketed for Alaskan Cruise Lines with ports of call in Vancouver, Seattle, Los Angeles, and San Diego, cruise liner boarding will be available in approximately thirty minutes. This is a short port of call, and the ship will be leaving this evening at 9:00 PM."

When the four got off the bus, Fran pressed and said, "Steven, what have you got planned?"

"We're going to Seattle," replied Steven.

"And just how are we going to do that?" Fran asked curiously.

Steven just pointed to the cruise ship without saying a word.

"How are we going to board a cruise ship without

tickets?"

"We just have to wait for the right opportunity," Steven replied.

"This is crazy, Steven," Fran said with every apprehension in the world.

Nonetheless, she would go along with Steven's plan, whatever it might be. As she saw it, at this point, they seemed to be out of options.

Steven pointed out to Fran the cargo loading area at the rear of the ship. At the moment, the door was open, and there was a forklift near the entrance. Oddly enough, there didn't appear to be anyone near the cargo door, at least no one on the outside, anyway.

Steven told Fran, "Our chance may be right now."

The four of them headed toward the open cargo door toward the rear of the ship, being careful to stay close to the ship to avoid being seen by those aboard the deck. As they approached the area near the cargo door, there were signs along the dock that read "RESTRICTED AREA".

Joshua said, "I don't think we're supposed to be here."

"Just come on, Joshua," Steven said rather emphatically.

Joshua complied, although it was obvious he didn't want to.

Upon approaching the cargo door, Steven was careful to look around again.

Not seeing anyone around, Steven just said, "Follow me."

Fran motioned for the boys to follow her, and all four of them made their way through the ship's cargo door. Once the four of them boarded the ship, they could see that the cargo area was rather large, somewhat like a warehouse. There seemed to be only one person in this area, quite a way away from them. Toward the left of them was a metal staircase. Steven figured he had one chance to get this right, and he motioned for the four of them to follow him up the stairs, even though he didn't know what awaited him on the other side of the door at the top. Amazingly, both boys made it to the top behind Steven and Fran without making a sound. Perhaps they were purposely being careful, however, Fran attributed this little successful venture to the boys being scared out of their minds.

The door at the top of the staircase had a latch on it. Steven opened the latch and the four went through the door. They were fortunate that Steven held the door open as the three passed through because when Steven carefully shut the door, it automatically locked behind them. One quick glance around, and both Steven and Fran could see that they were now in a corridor that had doors on each side of it that were labeled, "Private Ship Personnel Only". Steven couldn't help but to take a quick peek through the small window in the door of one of the rooms, and he quickly discovered that these rooms were the ship's personnel's private quarters. The four of them made their way down the corridor, with Fran, Joshua, and Justin following Steven, though Fran thought Steven had no idea where he was going. Nonetheless, Fran and the boys followed him. Just as they reached the end of the corridor and were about to go through another door, Steven could see a door on the right side that read "Supplies. Authorized Personnel Only". Steven pushed on the door in an attempt to open it, but it appeared to be locked.

Fran said, "Pull up on the lever."

"What lever?" replied Steven.

"The lever next to the latch," Fran said as she reached over Steven's arm to lift it herself and thinking that sometimes Steven was just as helpless as the boys.

The door opened, and the four of them went through it and discovered a room about the same size, or even a little larger than, one of the crew member's cabins. It certainly could not be called a closet by any means.

"What are you thinking?" Fran asked Steven.

"I'm thinking this would be a good spot to hold up until we get to Seattle," Steven replied.

"Are you kidding?"

"Fran, we really can't take a chance on being seen. We're not exactly ticketed passengers."

Fran was not happy about this decision, though she knew Steven was right. Knowing that the four of them would some how have to make do here, Fran made good use of the clean uniforms. It seemed enough of them put together made a good bed for each of them. Time passed, and eventually the ship departed from Sitka. The boys were starting to get hungry already, and Fran asked Steven what his plans were for food. Just as she said that, the door to the room opened. All four of them got very quiet. They had chosen an area out of the way of what they thought would be where people might be in and out, but that was no guarantee that they wouldn't be discovered. They could see just a pair of legs from where they were. They all remained as still as they could, and in just a couple of minutes, though it seemed like an eternity, the man left and closed the door behind him. Steven though it best that they stay there rather than venture out to scrounge for food, so hungry or not, they stayed where they were for the time being.

The next morning, the four of them woke up about the same time, something unusual for the Fruskin family, when Joshua and Justin both exclaimed, "I'm hungry."

Afterward, Fran just said, "Me too."

Steven knew he had to find some food somewhere, so he decided to venture outside the supply room to see what he could find. As he began to open the door, a man in a ship's uniform pushed on the door from the other side.

"What are you doing?" the man asked in an accent that was hardly recognizable. Not only was his accent hard to understand, but he also spoke rather abruptly.

Still, Steven was able to make out his question, and he answered the man, "We did stow away, but we had no choice."

"We?" the man asked, obviously attempting to get Steven to reveal the other people he was traveling with.

Knowing they had been discovered, Fran stood up with Joshua and Justin following suit.

"Your family?"

"Yes, this is my wife, Fran, and my sons, Joshua and Justin."

The man looked at Steven and said rapidly in his heavy accent, "I give you one chance. I like what you say, you stay."

So, once gain, Steven relayed their story to another person, this time not quite as detailed in an effort to compress quite a bit into a reasonable amount of time. The man listened intently as Steven spoke, and it seemed as though he could somehow empathize with Steven's situation.

When Steven finished speaking, the man said, "I help you."

Somewhat relieved, however still apprehensive, Steven waited in anticipation to hear what the man would say next.

He didn't have to wait long, as the next thing the man said was, "Come with me."

Steven motioned to Fran, Joshua, and Justin to come along with them, which was really meant to be an indication to the three that it was okay to go with the man. The man led the four to an empty personnel cabin. This cabin had four beds, two bunks on each side of it. It was small, however, it was a whole lot more than they had right now.

"You stay here. I bring you food," the man said as he left the cabin and shut the door behind them.

A short while later, the man returned to the cabin with a large platter containing fresh fruits and vegetables, sliced deli meats and cheeses, and a couple of different kinds of breads.

Still cautious about the mans intentions, Steven asked him, "Why are you helping us?"

"Like you. I too was a fugitive from my own government. They would say one thing to the people and do another thing. When I told the people of these things they do, my government came after me, like your government come after you. I flee my country. I think you are fool to return, but because I miss my home country, I help you," the man said in response.

The four of them were more than happy to have the food that the man brought them. Fran made sandwiches out of the bread meat and cheese, and after the four of them ate, they each found their own way of entertaining themselves, as they were unable to leave the cabin. Over the course of the next five days, the man continued to bring them food. The bathroom in the cabin included a small shower, and their host, who eventually introduced himself as Hassim, was kind enough to do their laundry for them and bring back fresh clean clothes. Eventually, the ship reached the port of Seattle, and even at the risk of losing his job, Hassim found it in his heart to find a way to successfully escort the four off the ship.

Now in Seattle, Steven's plan was to find his other brother and his family who lived somewhere near Bryars Sound. Steven had discussed with Fran what his plans were while they were still on the cruise ship, so the four of them set out on their quest to find Nelson, Steven's youngest brother. Their first stop was a public library to make use of a computer and try and locate Nelson. With a few simple directions from passers-by, they were successful in finding the library. When Steven asked to use one of the library's computers, he was told he had to have a library card.

Knowing that he could not fill out the library's form, for fear of being discovered by law enforcement agencies, Steven just said in a frustrated voice, "Forget it."

Fran had seen this type of behavior from Steven all too often, and she was used to dealing with it.

Steven looked at Fran and said, "What do we do now?"

Fran responded in her usual fashion and told Steven, "Just quit worrying."

She then asked the librarian lady behind the desk if they had a phone book. The lady handed Fran two rather thick books, one listing businesses, the other listing private residences.

Fran looked at Steven and said, "How many Nelson Fruskins could there be in Seattle anyway?" as she turned the pages in the phone book to the names listed under the letter "F". As it turned out, she was about to discover there were three. The first read "Fruskin, N.", the second "Fruskin, Nelson

A.", and the third, "Fruskin, Nelson F."

"What's your brother's middle name?" Fran asked Steven.

Steven replied, "Frank. Why?"

"2173 Cottonwood Boulevard," Fran answered confidently, in effect, saying, "I told you so."

Steven used the last of the money the pastor had given him to pay the fare for a cab from the library to the address they had found in the phone book. When they arrived at their destination, they discovered that it was an apartment complex. They headed to the office, but when Steven inquired about where his brother lived, the manager told him that he could not give out that information, as it would violate the company privacy policy. Steven and Fran resigned themselves to the fact that they would have to wait at the entrance to the complex in hopes of seeing Nelson leaving or returning.

They didn't have to wait long. It was only about forty-five minutes when, as Steven and Fran were talking to each other, a car pulled up next to them on the way out of the complex.

As the he rolled down the window, the driver said, "What are you doing here?"

Immediately recognizing the driver as his brother, Steven answered Nelson, "We need your help."

"Look, I have an appointment, but you can wait in the apartment. Shannon and the kids are there. It's number 205 in building 12. I'll be back soon."

Steven, Fran, Justin, and Joshua walked to the apartment and knocked on the door. Nelson had already called Shannon, and when she opened the door, she invited the four in. After a few short hugs, the conversation turned to the experiences the four of them had recently been through. Although it had been at least an hour before Nelson returned to the apartment, it seemed as though it had only been minutes.

When he did returned, he offered Fran a short hug and shook his brother's hand, saying, "Long time no see."

Steven answered, "Yeah, I know."

"You know there are people looking for you."

"I know."

"Steven, can I ask you a question? What the hell does the Department of Justice want with you and Fran anyway?"

"Well, it's a long story. Kind of interesting actually."

Shannon chimed in, "Oh, it's interesting alright." So while the girls talked, Steven and Nelson went out on the balcony to talk.

After Steven told Nelson of their experiences over the past few months, Nelson replied, "Well, you know you can't stay here. They'll find you."

"Nelson, I'm tired of running," Steven said in a way that conveyed he was asking for help.

"Tell you what, Steven. You can stay here for a couple of days, until I figure things out." He explained that he thought it best that Steven, Fran, and the boys stay inside the apartment, as not to draw attention to themselves.

Steven agreed as he told Nelson, "That's no problem. Fran and the kids like it better inside anyway."

Joshua passed the time in his usual manner, working on his computer, while it didn't take Justin long to find a stash of video games and immediately ask Sharron if he could play them. Fran and Shannon spent the time just visiting with each other, largely talking about what most men would consider trivial matters.

A couple of evenings later, when Nelson returned home from work, he told Steven he had some good news. It turned out his boss owned a small cabin in the woods west of the city. The cabin was rather isolated and quite a drive from the city proper. Also, because of time constraints at work, Nelson's boss hasn't had time to take care of it the way he would like to. Nelson explained to his boss that he had family that needed a place to stay, and his boss agreed to rent the place to Nelson at a very nominal price, if he agreed to make sure the work that needed to be done actually got done.

Nelson told Steven, "No lease, no paperwork. Everything will be in my name. No one will know you're staying there, except me and my boss. You even kind of have a job."

"What job?" Steven asked.

"Think about it, Steven."

That was all Nelson had to say before it dawned on Steven that he would be the one fixing this place up, and if history was once again an indication of the future, for the most part, it would be just him fixing the place up. On the long drive up to the cabin, Nelson brought up the fact that it might be in Steven's, Fran's, Joshua's, and Justin's best interests if they were to consider changing their names, of course, bypassing the usual legal means of doing so. With some convincing from Nelson, Steven finally agreed to consider the possibility. After what must have been at least an hour and a half ride, and a trip that included a trek down several dirt roads, they arrived at the cabin.

The first words Fran said were, "Oh my God."

"It's not that bad," replied Steven.

The metal roof on the one-story cabin had a piece missing off of it on the right side, and the rest of the roof was covered in leaves. One of the posts holding up the porch on the front of the cabin looked like it was about to fall down, and the area immediately surrounding the cabin was overgrown with tall weeds. One might wonder how such type of vegetation could grow in this terrain, but no matter, Steven obviously had his work cut out for him.

Steven looked at Fran and said, "Come on, let's check it out."

The cabin looked small on the outside, however, when they made their way inside, they discovered that it had two bedrooms, as well as a living room and kitchen, although the latter could be considered one room. There was even a full bath with a tub type shower. The cabin was furnished and even had minimal supplies in the cupboards. As Fran stood in the kitchen, she ran the tap in the sink out of curiosity and discovered that although the pressure seemed very light, the water certainly was clear. Nelson commented that he believed the water supply was from a spring-fed well.

Justin asked, "Where's the TV?"

"You don't need TV," replied Steven.

Justin responded, in a tone indicating that life wasn't worth living without a TV, "Yeah I do."

It didn't take but a minute for Joshua to realize there was not a computer either, but he was content with his laptop. For now, this is where the four would stay.

Chapter 28

After a series of stalls by both the U.S. and Canadian Governments, negotiations between the two countries with regards to Steven's, Fran's, Joshua's, and Justin's fates finally resumed after about two months. The same members of the previous delegations from both countries were once again present for continued negotiations.

In light of the fact that these proceedings were taking place in Canada, the same man who was originally acting as Canada's spokesman during the last session of negotiations began to speak once again, "Gentlemen, I see no need to rehash the events of our last meeting. We all know why we're here, so let's get right down to business. After conferring with those individuals within my government who's decisions are relevant to these proceedings, the Canadian Government has agreed to a joint investigation with both the U.S. and Canadian law enforcement agencies with the strict stipulation that Steven, Fran, Joshua, and Justin not be extradited to the United States."

A spokesman with the U.S. Department of Justice replied, "Mr. Speaker, I believe I speak for the entire delegation when I say that the proposal you are speaking of is unacceptable to the U.S. Government, or for that matter, any U.S. agency involved in this investigation."

"Well, then, gentlemen, I believe we're at square one."

"I don't think so, Mr. Speaker." As the man spoke, it was obvious he was now addressing everyone in the room, "The purpose of the recess of these negotiations at our last session was to authorize an agreement with both countries to establish a venue for joint investigation with the United States and Canada in the tracking and apprehension of Steven, Fran, Joshua, and Justin Fruskin. I believe both of our governments have agreed to the joint investigation, although we may not agree on the course of action taken once the investigation has reached a point where its objective has been accomplished. It is my belief that it would be in the best interest of both our nations if we moved forward at the moment. We can hash out our differences in what we believe should be the final results of this investigation when the time comes."

A representative from Canada's Royal Canadian Mounted Police working at the federal level responded, "I'm inclined to agree. I believe, at the moment, both of our countries are in agreement with relevance to the immediate objective set before us. I'm sure all of us in this room, along with the powers that be on both sides, can agree that it is in all of our best interest to proceed with a joint investigation at this point. I'm sure it is obvious that the sooner we have these four back in a controllable environment, the less damage control will be necessary from either of our governments."

Jason Culver, Canada's Minister of Public Safety simply responded, "I concur."

A representative from the Federal Bureau of Investigation on the U.S. side now made an attempt to take the proceedings in a slightly different direction, as he believed the matter had been resolved, at least for the moment anyway.

He began to speak, "Gentlemen, I'm certain it is obvious to everyone in this room that agencies from both countries have certainly continued their investigation with regards to the Fruskin case over the last two months. I'm sure we would all agree that it certainly would be beneficial to all of us if we could find it in our hearts to reveal what we have learned up to this point."

"I would be inclined to agree," another representative of the U.S. Delegation said, in an obvious attempt to get Canada's Delegation to reveal any new knowledge with respect to the Fruskin case.

A spokesman for Canada's Public Affairs answered,

"Perhaps it would be in the best interest of everyone here to allow the U.S. Delegation to speak to that matter, since the latest results of our investigation seem to indicate that the four we are all so desperately seeking are no longer in Canada. As a matter of fact, if our latest intelligence is correct, I believe these four may actually be in the United States."

"What makes you so certain of that?" asked a representative from the U.S. Delegation.

Canada's representative answered the question, "Sir, over the years, I have learned that the word 'certainty' is an objective term; however, I can tell you that I have complete confidence in the Canadian agencies responsible for collecting such data to ensure that the information they have is credible before submitting it to their superiors. Perhaps it would be beneficial to hear what the United States and its agencies have learned with regards to this case."

With that being said, the representative from the U.S. Department of Justice felt obligated to speak to the Canadian representative's statement, though cautiously.

He began, "I would like to take this opportunity to address the entire Canadian Delegation, if I may. It is certainly obvious if both our countries are to proceed with a joint investigation with regards to the Fruskin case, all of the agencies with respect to both countries must feel an obligation to share information they have obtained with the agencies deemed appropriate to continue with this investigation. With that in mind, I feel obliged to inform you that according to latest intelligence compiled by U.S. agencies, we can assure the Canadian Government that the U.S. has entertained the possibility that the Fruskins may no longer be within Canada's national border."

At this point, Jason Culver stood up and said, "Gentlemen, it is obvious that we clearly have issues that need to be addressed when it comes to reaching a successful resolution with regards to these negotiations. Based on what I've heard today, I can only hope that those who are involved in this investigation at what I would refer to as a 'street level' are much more proactive when it comes to sharing the information deemed necessary to accomplish both our countries' objectives with respect to this case, namely, the successful apprehension of Steven, Fran, Joshua, and Justin Fruskin. Although this session of negotiations was rather short in length, both countries agreed that the immediate objective they had set out to accomplish had been reached, and for the time being, no further benefit could come as a result of continuing the negotiations at this point."

With that being said, both the U.S. and Canadian Delegations agreed to adjourn until such time it was deemed appropriate to reconvene.

Chapter 29

Thus began what would be a long joint investigation with some of the highest level law enforcement agencies in both Canada and the United States. Remarkably, Agent Benson was still with the U.S. Department of Justice, and when he was offered the opportunity to participate in a joint investigation with the U.S. and Canada in an effort to find and apprehend Steven, Fran, Joshua, and Justin Fruskin, it took no time at all for him to seize it and agree to work directly with Canadian law enforcement officials in an effort to find these four. Agent Benson soon found himself on a plane headed for Ottawa for a prearranged meeting with Jason Culver to be briefed on what information Canada had compiled on the Fruskin case, at least the information that Canada was willing to share. When Agent Benson arrived at the airport in Ottawa, he was met by Canadian officials from the office of Canada's Minister of Public Safety and subsequently transported to a predesignated location where this meeting was to take place.

The building where the meeting took place was rather upscale, something Agent Benson was not accustomed to; however, likely selected to purposely appear out of the norm. The entrance to the building consisted of two tall glass double doors with brass finished handles. The floor was made of a marble-like material, and there was a large stone fountain in the center of the lobby. Two staircases on each side of the lobby led to a loft that was spotted with artificial trees.

The Canadian officials Agent Benson met at the airport led him up the staircase on the left and down a hallway that had tall wooden doors on both sides of it. At the very end of the hallway, there was a set of double doors. One of the Canadian officials scanned a card through a reader that was mounted on the wall to the right of the door. Once inside, there was a counter immediately on the right and a hallway, at the end of the counter, that led to offices on each side of the room. The Canadian officials escorting Agent Benson showed the girl behind the counter their identification and continued to walk toward the hallway, escorting Agent Benson to the right at the end of the counter. The doors on each side of the hallway all had security pads next to them. One of the Canadian officials punched in a four digit code on the keypad next to the third door on the right. The door unlocked, and the three of them went inside.

The room was nothing more than a small office with a desk on the left and a set of chairs against the wall toward the right. There was another door directly behind the desk. When the three entered, there was no one in the room. It didn't take long for someone to come through the door behind the desk. The man introduced himself to Agent Benson as Jason Culver, Canada's Minister of Public Safety.

Jason began to speak to Agent Benson, "I understand you've been following the Fruskin case in the U.S.?"

"I have," replied Agent Benson.

"Perhaps you can tell me what you've learned in the course of your investigation."

"Mr. Culver, I know who you are. I respect your position and the wealth of knowledge I'm sure you have gained over the years. However, I'm fully aware that both the U.S. and Canada feel it is in their best interest to share only the information they deem to be necessary to divulge in order to reach the objective set forth by each of our governments. That being said, I believe you'll find that I personally will be a hell of a lot easier to work with if we can leave the political rhetoric out of this."

"Fair enough. Let me share with you what we have learned up to this point." At that point, Mr. Culver pulled up a video on a laptop that appeared to be footage recorded from a police dash camera.

After watching the video, Agent Benson asked Jason, "What am I watching here?"

"This video was recorded from a police dash cam on a routine traffic stop in the Yukon territory. We believe this is the last known contact with the Fruskins by Canadian law enforcement."

"How can you be sure these people were the Fruskins?"

"The driver was positively identified as Jerry Fruskin. Our Mountie suspected something wasn't quite right, however, he had no legal recourse to hold them."

"Mr. Culver, it seems strange to me that your border patrol agents were successful in detaining the Fruskins, but an officer with the RCMP was not able to find the legal means necessary to detain them. I may not be familiar with Canadian law, but my gut instinct is telling me that your officer just screwed up!"

"Agent Benson, you have my assurance that everyone affiliated with this office, including myself, will give any member of U.S. law enforcement involved with this case the respect that they deserve. I would ask that you do the same."

"Dually noted. Where do we go from here?"

"Our intelligence tells us that the four of them may have crossed the border back into the U.S. somewhere in southeast Alaska from the Yukon territory."

"Mr. Culver, if you knew these four were now in the U.S., why didn't you just share that information with the appropriate U.S. law enforcement agency. Don't tell me. Let me guess. This was your government's way of ensuring that Canadian law enforcement was kept actively involved in this investigation."

"You're free to believe what you perceive, Agent Benson. However, with regards to matters at hand, there is a plane waiting for you at the Ottowa airport. You and these gentlemen next to you will be flying to Fairbanks. We will fill you in with further details on the plane. I am certain you will make every effort to cooperate with our agents during the course of this investigation."

"Pleasure to meet you, sir."

The three of them left the office and headed for the Ottowa airport. Once arriving at the airport, the three of them boarded a Canadian airliner bound for Fairbanks. Over the course of the six hour flight, the Canadian agents were kind enough to fill Agent Benson in on further details that Canadian intelligence had provided them. It didn't take long for Agent Benson to realize that this was obviously credible information, and it would certainly be in his best interest to share what he had learned over the course of his investigation if he was going to continue to obtain the information he needed from the Canadian agents in order to continue his investigation. Once landing in Fairbanks, one of the Canadian agents rented a car from a rental agency at the airport. When Agent Benson inquired of the Canadian agent why they were not utilizing local U.S. law enforcement for their transportation needs, he was told that it was important that they maintain a low profile and any indication of local law enforcement could very well hinder their investigation. After an overnight stay in Fairbanks, the three of them got off to an early start and began the long drive toward the small town of Stewart, where Canadian intelligence had indicated this was the last place the Fruskins had been seen.

It seemed as though this was going to be where the real joint investigation would actually begin. Both the Canadian agents and Agent Benson could only hope that, as information was acquired from any member on the team, that it would be shared with every member on the team. After nearly a nine-hour drive to the tiny town of Stewart, the three pulled into the parking lot of the same little store where the church van had stopped with the Fruskins. It didn't take much more than a quick inquiry by one of the Canadian agents inside the store to discover that the clerk indeed did remember seeing Joshua and Justin Fruskin. Once learning that they were with the driver of the church van, the three of them headed for the church at the edge of town. When they arrived at the church, it was locked up tighter than a drum, and the three thought it best that they find a place to stay for the evening. They found what basically was a small bed and breakfast in town and booked a room there for the evening. The next morning, the three returned to the church.

When Agent Benson inquired of Pastor Trevers what he had learned during the course of his interactions with the Fruskins, Pastor Trevers replied, "Agent Benson, I'm afraid I have a moral obligation to keep matters my parishioners disclose to me in confidentiality just that, confidential."

"Mr. Trevers, does the fact that what you consider protecting the confidentiality of your parishioners we interpret as hindering a U.S. federal investigation, and I believe my colleagues here would agree that you would also be hindering an international investigation, bother you at all?"

"I believe I have an obligation to answer to an authority that myself and many others in my profession believe supersedes the authority of any government agency."

At that point, Agent Benson looked at the two Canadian agents to gain assurance that what he was about to do was something they both agreed with.

With a nod of agreement from both the Canadian agents, Agent Benson looked at Pastor Trevers and said, "Mr. Trevers, you are being placed under arrest for hindering a U.S. federal investigation with additional charges pending for hindering a U.S./Canadian joint investigation."

Pastor Trevers was instructed to place his hands behind his back as Agent Benson cuffed him. Unfortunately for Agent Benson and his Canadian counterparts, they were now forced to involve local law enforcement, something they had hoped to avoid. Agent Benson contacted the nearest outpost of the Alaskan state troopers, and they were met by a trooper who happened to be working in the area. The pastor was transported to Fairbanks while Agent Benson and his Canadian colleagues continued to question local residents, seeking information that would provide them a trail to follow in search of the Fruskins. They soon learned that the local congregation had raised enough money to buy a bus ticket to send the Fruskins to Sitka.

When Agent Benson and the Canadian agents learned of the purchase of the bus ticket, their next step was to begin the long drive to a small town in the northern part of Alaska's southeastern panhandle with the intention of obtaining further transportation to Sitka by means of a private helicopter. Unfortunately for Agent Benson and the Canadian agents, bypassing the Alaskan Marine Highway could very well turn out to be a crucial mistake. They would soon find out that the decision would cause them to sacrifice gaining knowledge of events that took place which would lead them further in the right direction. This would turn out to be a sixteen hour drive for these three. Although the agents believed that they would have an opportunity to further their investigation along the way, it would seem that everyone they questioned had no knowledge of the Fruskins passing through anytime recently, or for that matter, at all.

After two days of driving and staying overnight in another small bed and breakfast, the agents finally arrived in the town of Haines, Alaska. From here they chartered a private helicopter to fly them to Sitka. Working with the Sitka police department, upon questioning the agent at the Sitka bus station, the agents soon learned that the Fruskins were indeed there, and that the bus agent had allowed the Fruskins to return to the port where the ferry had originally docked.

When the agents arrived at the port, there was no ship docked; however, a conversation with the security guard there revealed that a cruise liner from Alaskan Cruise Lines would have been docked at the port right about the times the Fruskins would have returned. When the agents learned of this, they questioned the security guard with regards to what type of security system was in place at the port. The guard explained that security basically consisted of himself, an alarm system for the building on the dock, and cameras inside and outside the building. With the guards help, the agents conducted a review of the cameras at the dock that would allow them to monitor the area during the time it was believed that the Fruskins would have been there. The port's security system was old, but still effective. After reviewing tape after tape, Agent Benson thought he saw what he was looking for. He instructed the guard to rewind the tape. When it was replayed, sure enough, the camera on the outside of the port building had recorded the Fruskins boarding the cruise liner through the ship's cargo door. Both agent Benson and the Canadian agents felt this was the break in the case they needed. They would soon find out that the next steps in their investigation would not quite take the path they anticipated.

When the agents contacted Alaskan Cruise Lines, they were told that the Fruskins were not listed on the passenger manifest list. With some difficulty, the agents were finally able to explain to the cruise liner representative that the Fruskins would not appear on the passenger manifest list, and what they were really interested in were the images captured by the ship's elaborate camera system. Alaskan Cruise Lines was less than thrilled with the idea of complying with that request. They felt that even entertaining the idea may, in fact, open up a floodgate of possible impending litigation. Of course, when Agent Benson explained that refusing their request could only result in litigation of a federal nature, representatives from the cruise liner's legal department stated that they had full intentions of cooperating with U.S. authorities in every aspect of their investigation, but they had an ongoing commitment to protect the rights and best interest of their passengers, past, future, and present. Alaskan Cruise Lines believed one of those rights was a reasonable expectation of privacy. Thus began what Agent Benson knew would be a lengthy court battle that would only serve to stall his investigation, with the time frame for its outcome limited only by the amount of money Alaskan Cruise Lines was willing to spend.

Chapter 30

It would seem that Alaskan Cruise Lines resolve to protect their best interest was exactly the break that the Fruskins needed to regain some normalcy in their lives. The four of them spent the next few months in Steven's brother's boss's cabin. With the equipment and tools Nelson was kind enough to provide, Steven was able to transform the cabin and the land around it into something Nelson's boss would enjoy staying in. Needless to say, Fran once again found a way to make the place home, but she knew in her heart they could not stay there. Justin was not in school, and she actually felt guilty that Joshua's life had been interrupted for their sake. As time passed, Fran's feelings on the matter intensified, and Steven was certainly able to pick up on it. It was unusual for Steven not to ask Fran what was wrong when he suspected something, but, this time, he refrained. Perhaps it was because he felt he knew what the issue was, and he had come to like the place he was living in. After all, it had always been his dream to own a small cabin in the woods, and although he didn't own it, his surroundings were extremely comfortable to him.

Fran had expected that Steven would pick up on her discontent and eventually ask her what was wrong so she could give him her usual answer consisting of that, by now famous, one word, "Nothing", fully expecting Steven to know darn well what was wrong, giving them both a chance to talk about the issue. When Steven didn't ask, Fran felt it important to take it upon herself to let him know how she felt.

Late one evening, as the two were preparing to go to bed, before turning out the light, Fran turned to look at Steven and just said, "We can't stay here, you know."

Fran fully expected Steven to reply with the words, "Why not," but that didn't happen. Her statement had opened up Stevens mind to the very real possibility that staying in one place too long would only lead inevitably to law enforcement finding them, which was exactly what Fran was thinking, though she really wanted to find a place they could just stay. She had no idea how that was going to come about, and she needed Steven's help in doing so.

Much to Fran's surprise, Steven replied, "I know."

That answer wasn't enough for Fran, and she replied, "Steven, we have to talk about this."

Steven replied, "In the morning," and rolled over and turned out the light.

Fran just lied there for a minute, didn't say anything, then turned out the light and rolled as far over to her edge of the bed as she could, in an obvious attempt to convey her discontent to Steven. This was her silent way of telling Steven, "Don't touch me." This behavior was rather rare from her. Nevertheless, it would rear its ugly head from time to time, especially when she was extremely discontent with Steven's actions.

The next morning, when Fran woke up, Steven was already outside, working on splitting some logs for firewood. There was already a rather large pile of wood split, and Fran suspected this was Steven's way of releasing some pent up anger.

Eventually, Steven came inside, and much to Fran's surprise, the first words out of his mouth were, "Fran, you're right. We can't stay here."

Fran replied, "What are we going to do Steven?"

"I think Nelson is right. The only way we're going to stop running and get our lives back is to change our names."

"How are we going to do that? We can't go to court for a name change."

"I didn't say we were going to do it legally."

"Steven, not again!"

"Don't worry, we're not going to have to keep doing this

forever. Who knows? Maybe this will be the last time."

"I hope so. I hope so," replied Fran in a voice indicating she was just tired of all of this.

The very next day, Steven contacted his brother Nelson, in an attempt to see if he could help him with regards to the matter at hand. After all, a name change was Nelson's idea anyway. As it turned out, Nelson had recently worked on a claim where he remembered a single mother telling him her son had recently been arrested for trying to purchase alcoholic beverages with a fake ID. She had told Nelson that she felt the cops had no right to arrest her son on that charge because the ID that was in his possession was actually a state-issued ID from the DMV. It was more the manner in which he obtained the ID that was in question. Apparently the paperwork necessary to obtain the ID was what was actually in question. Her son obtained that from a friend in high school. It was her belief that if her son didn't try to buy the beer, none of this would have happened. The only reason the clerk questioned the ID was because her son was obviously under the age of twenty-one. Nelson returned to the sight of the original claim and explained to the boy's mother that because the claim had involved her son's car when she hit the house, whether her son was driving at the time or not, he still needed to talk to her son in order to finalize the claim. She was more than happy to oblige. Nelson was rather careful with his conversation, arranging his line of questioning and comments in just the right order to lead into his true purpose for his visit, obtaining the information he needed with regards to how he might be able to put them in contact with his friend in order to round up the paperwork they needed to obtain the valid ID's they needed.

The teen responded, "Look, bro, if you want my bud to hook you up with a chalked ID, I can hook you up. Fake docs, no can do. Gonna cost you though. Two Benjamins a chalk."

"Are you out of your mind. That's eight hundred dollars."

"Supply and demand, bro. Supply and demand."

Nelson knew that his brother was in a desperate spot, so

after talking to Steven, and the two of them agreeing that this was meant to be a loan to be paid back when he could, Nelson found it in his heart to cough up the money for the ID's. Nelson was rather cautious with the venture down this path with the wrong side of the law, and he alone accompanied the teen to his friends place, where the transaction was to take place. The new ID's had to have different names. However, Steven though it best that the new names sounded close to their old names, and he had already provided Nelson with the new names for the ID's. Fran Fruskin would now be Felecia Fryers, while Joshua would become Jonathan Freyers and Justin would go by Jason Fryers. Steven would assume the name Sean Fryers. Steven didn't much care for the name Sean, but he knew it was important to choose a name that sounded close to his old one. After Nelson and the teen made the cash exchange portion of the transaction, Nelson had the new IDs in his hand within the week.

Chapter 31

After a long, heartfelt conversation, Nelson and Steven, now Sean, both thought it best to relocate to another state and begin a new life with his family as the Freyers. Sean's first order of business was to find employment in another state, preferably in the southwest, as Sean thought this was the least likely place law enforcement would be looking for them. Sean scoured the websites on Nelson's computer for a job posting that was in a field he was familiar with. He sent off applications with his newly created resume as an attachment. In the days that followed, Sean continued this process, with the mindset that the more applications he had out there, the better the odds of finding employment.

Toward the beginning of the following week, Sean now found himself on the phone with several recruiters from different companies to schedule initial interviews by phone. As Sean found himself on the phone with representatives from different companies for initial screening interviews, most set up an interview with those individuals from each of those companies for further evaluation. Fortunately for Sean, most of these further interviews were all in one state. Sean now needed to plan a trip to southern California to accommodate his obligation for each of these interviews. In a bold move, he had asked the interviewers to schedule each of his interviews in the same week, thereby allowing him to make the needed travel plans.

Once again, Nelson found it in his heart to accommodate his brother with the needed funds to make this trip, knowing that, in the greater scheme of things, his actions would only serve to return his brother and his brother's family to some sort of normalcy. When Sean talked to his wife about making the trip to California, as usual, when it came to matters that involved major changes in the course of her husband's career, she was more than supportive. She knew he had to make the trip alone.

When the time came, Nelson took Sean to the airport, where he had the opportunity to try out his new ID in a real life situation, as he needed it for check-in, to go through security, and to receive his boarding pass. He was careful to think of things that would cause him to be less nervous for each of these interactions. Perhaps this method of thinking was the right idea because he managed to pass through all three and board the plane. He took his seat on the plane, feeling relieved he had made it there. Of course, staying true to his usual paranoid personality, he thought to himself he wasn't in the air yet. The door to the plane was closed, and the massive jet began to taxi toward the runway. When the jet reached the runway, the plane stopped. After about a minute, Sean could hear the roar of the engines as it prepared for takeoff. It didn't take long before the jet was speeding down the runway, and Sean could feel his back press against the seat. Soon, the jet was in the air, and Sean was on his way to southern California.

Once Sean was comfortable with the fact that the possibility of any interruption to his flight plans now didn't exist, he chose to make good use of his time over the course of the nearly three-hour flight by reviewing the papers he had printed out from his brother's computer. Each set of papers contained information on the history of the companies he had interviews with. Sean knew that the more he knew about a company, along with the right combination of experience, and a positive attitude, the more likely it would give him an edge over other applicants interviewing for the same position. As the flight neared its end, the flight attendant made the standard landing announcement.

Sean expected that the city of Los Angeles would be rather large, but the sheer mass of it was a wonder to see from above. He made his way through the airport and to a rental car agency he had chosen. Once again, he presented his ID, and with no problems being detected, he was now becoming rather confident that the ID he had in his possession would serve its purpose. After obtaining his rental car, he drove to the hotel he had made online reservations with. Although he seemed to have a tendency toward keeping things simple in life, the rental car's on board navigation system was a welcome sight, especially in a city he was unfamiliar with.

When Sean arrived at the hotel, upon checking in, the desk clerk asked for his ID, which he provided. After handing the ID back, the desk clerk asked him to fill out a card with his information and vehicle plate number. Once that was complete, Sean handed the card back and the desk clerk asked for a credit card to secure the room. Sean asked the desk clerk why she needed a credit card when the room had already been paid for in full online. She explained it was necessary to secure incidental charges. Frustrated, Sean pulled out of his wallet the same credit card he had been using for years. The desk clerk did not check the card against Sean's ID, as she had already handed it back to him.

When the desk clerk ran the card, she handed it back to Sean and said, "I'm sorry, Mr. Fruskin. The computer is asking for an alternate ID."

Sean knew immediately what he had done, and he apologized and handed the desk clerk the prepaid credit card he had purchased earlier. After running the card, the desk clerk handed Sean a room key card, and gave him directions to the room. The room was comfortable, and it afforded Sean an opportunity to get some rest before his first interview the next morning. Sean called the front desk for a wake-up call and also set the alarm on his newly purchased cellphone.

When morning came, Sean grabbed a quick breakfast from the buffet set up by the hotel and then got an early start toward his first interview. Once again, the rental car's on board navigational system came in handy, and Sean arrived for his interview with time to spare. The building where the interview was to take place was only about ten stories high and lacked the usual elegance of taller buildings. Sean's interview was on the seventh floor, and as he made his way to the elevator, he tried to fight the usual nervousness that came with an impending interview. When he opened the door to the office down the hall from the elevator, the receptionist desk was directly in front of him. The lady behind the desk was young, maybe in her early twenties, with long blond hair, and she obviously took care of herself. Sean was careful not to stare and introduced himself as Sean Freyers.

The young lady responded, "Yes, I see you have an eleven o' clock with Mr. Dobson. Just have a seat right over there, and I'll let you know when you can go on back."

Sean took a seat and patiently waited for his scheduled interview.

It wasn't long, and soon a taller gentleman, relatively thin, in his late-forties, and very well-dressed, came into the waiting area and looked at Sean and said, "Mr. Freyers, come on back."

Sean followed the man down a hall and into a very large office, where the man asked him to have a seat. He introduced himself as Jack Dobson and gave a brief summary of his intended structure for the impending interview, obviously to set Sean at ease.

After verifying some personal information, the first thing Mr. Dobson said was, "So, tell me what you know about our company."

Sean's prior initiative to learn about each of the companies he had interviews with was about to pay off. He told the interviewer what he knew, including a brief history of the company, their product lines, the company's most recent success, and even the names of the company's top executives. This set the tone for the interview, as Sean could tell that Mr. Dobson was obviously impressed. Jack continued with some questions regarding Sean's work history, and the interview turned into something that was rather lengthy, always a good sign. When Sean left, he felt confident it went well. He had time to grab a quick bite before driving to the only other interview scheduled for the day.

Upon arriving at his destination for the second interview, Sean made his way up the stairs to the second story of the three-story building. Sean thought it odd that the building didn't have an elevator, and he had a gut feeling something wasn't quite right. Once again, upon opening the door to the office where the interview was to take place, he was met by a receptionist who he introduced himself to. The receptionist asked him to take a seat and let him know that his interviewer would be out shortly. It wasn't too long, and soon, Sean was met by a taller lady with long, straight, sandy brown hair, professionally dressed, probably in her mid-twenties, and obviously someone who was very careful about maintaining her appearance. She introduced herself as Dianne and asked Sean to followed her back to her office. This interview followed basically the same structure as Sean's prior interview, and although she tried to hide it, Sean could tell by Dianne's body languages that she seemed to be less than impressed with his qualifications. Add that to the fact that Dianne's responses were rather short, and sometimes what Sean felt were abrupt. He knew that this interview was not going well at all.

After what was a much shorter interview than the prior one, Dianne closed the interview with the all too common, "Well, Sean, we have some other applicants to interview, and if it turns out your qualifications best meet our needs, then we will be contacting you. Thank you for coming in."

Sean thanked Dianne for the opportunity to speak with her and left the office slightly saddened only at how the interview took the course it did, as he knew he was well qualified for the position. Something inside him, however, told him he didn't want to work there anyway. With that, he headed back to his hotel room, where he watched TV and ordered a pizza later. He didn't call his wife that evening, for reasons he felt were obvious. That did not stop her from calling him, though. When the phone rang, Sean answered with a "Hello" with a tone that implied he wondered who could possibly be calling him.

Sean immediately recognized the voice on the other end of the line as the first question that popped out was, "Well, how did it go?"

Sean immediately responded, "What are you doing calling me here? Someone could be listening."

Fran, who by now really should be going by Felecia, taking into account all that had happened to them in the past, responded, "Oh, don't be ridiculous, Steven. No one is listening to us. You're just paranoid."

Sean countered, "You shouldn't call me by that name. We need to use the names on our ID's."

"Steven, Steven, Steven," Fran responded in an effort to downplay Sean's concern over the issue. Although Fran thought what she said was funny, Sean failed to see the humor in her response. She gave into "Steven's" wishes, only because she wanted to have a pleasant conversation with her husband. If that was what it would take to do so, then this time, she would. The phone call only lasted for about fifteen minutes, as Sean told his wife, who for this conversation was now going by Felecia, about how his day went, and how he felt the interviews went. As he hung up the phone, he thought about how much he loved his wife; however, he was concerned that Fran was not taking their situation seriously enough. He resolved that when he returned to what was now serving as home for them, he would have to have a serious conversation with her on the seriousness of the situation, and what the possible implications could be if she and the rest of the family did not embrace what he felt was not only a new set of names, but basically the establishment of a new life for them.

Chapter 32

Sean finished out his week in southern California with the remaining interviews he had scheduled and soon found himself sitting on a plane bound for Seattle. The plane had not left the gate yet, and although Sean had once again made it through the busy airport, through security, and onto the plane, it still seemed that at every turn, Sean felt as though someone was going to stop him. He wanted so much to return his life, as well as the lives of his family, back to something that resembled a normal life for them, but he was now questioning whether he would ever be able to do that. As the plane backed away from the gate and headed down the tarmac towards the runway, Sean kept going over in his mind what the immediate future might hold for them. Every thought that went through his mind, however, was only speculation. Wanting to get his mind off such thoughts for the moment, he decided to make good use of the in-flight movie that was offered. The movie not only helped to make him feel more comfortable, but it also seemed to pass the time so quickly that he now found himself listening to an announcement stating that the plane was beginning its descent into Seattle.

Sean was met at the airport by his brother, who drove Sean back out to the cabin. Of course, Nelson asked Sean how he felt the interviews went, and he responded saying that there might be a couple of good prospects. Nelson indicated that he was glad to hear it, and the two filled the remainder of the time on their drive to the cabin with light conversation. When they finally arrived outside the cabin, they were met at the car by Jonathan and Jason. Sean asked where their mother was and was told she was inside cooking dinner. She was basically forced to do so now because the cabin they were living in was so far from civilization. When Sean walked into the cabin, he found his wife standing in front of the stove, stirring something in a pot. The cabin was filled with the aroma of hamburger cooking with onions, along with the smell of something Italian.

Felecia looked at Sean and said, "How did it go?" all the while never leaving the stove.

Sean had no intention of putting up with that and walked over to her, took the wooden spoon out of his wife's hands, and put his arms around her as she also embraced her husband. The two hugged for a moment or two. Jonathan and Jason pretended not to notice, though they were both secretly happy to see their parents back together again.

After dinner, and after the kids had went to bed, Sean looked at his wife and said, "Felecia, we have to talk."

She immediately pulled away from Sean, knowing exactly what the conversation was going to be about, and responded, "I don't like that name."

Sean asked, "What don't you like about it?"

Sean received exactly the response he was expecting, as the next thing she said was an emphatic, "I just don't."

"Look, sweetheart, you have to understand that it's necessary if we're going to put our lives back together. If I hadn't changed my name, I couldn't possibly have had the interviews I just had."

"How do you know that?"

"Think about it, sweetheart. They're still looking for us."

"You don't know that. It's been months."

"That isn't very long. I just want you guys to have a normal life again."

"That's what I want, too," Felecia said in a voice mixed with frustration and a heartfelt desire for it to come true.

"Then trust me on this."

She looked into Sean's eyes, with a hint of desire, and said, "Felecia, huh?"

Sean responded softly, yet firmly, "Felecia," and the

two shared a kiss.

Chapter 33

A couple of weeks passed, and late in the afternoon, the phone rang. Felecia answered it, and she immediately knew the call was of some importance, as the caller was asking for Sean Freyers. Felecia thought this had to be a representative from one of the companies Sean had visited in southern California. When Sean answered the phone, the voice inquired if he was indeed talking to Sean Freyers. Upon confirming that it was, the voice identified himself as Jack Dobson, the gentleman he had interviewed with at the very beginning of his week in California. He wanted to schedule another interview. Sean was somewhat excited about the prospect, while at the same time perplexed, as he had no idea how he could possibly afford another trip to southern California. Nelson had already been more than generous with his finances in an effort to help out his brother.

His fears were immediately put to rest, as Mr. Dobson said, "I realize another trip to southern California may not be an option at the moment, so what I'd like to do is schedule a phone interview with Mr. Trevors in our Human Resource department. It's really just a formality, as our company requires two interviews for this position."

Sean responded, "That would be great," already mulling over in his mind whether his response sounded to eager.

"Okay, I have an opening for 2:00 PM on Thursday this week. Will that work for you?"

"That would be fine," Sean responded in a more professional matter.

"OK, I have you confirmed for a 2:00 PM interview this Thursday with Mr. Trevors."

"I'll be looking forward to his call."

"Have a good evening, Mr. Freyers."

"Thank you. You, too," Sean said as he hung up the phone.

Felecia was listening the whole time, and as Sean hung up the phone, she asked, "Well?"

Sean responded, "I think I might have the job."

"What do you mean you think you might have the job. Do you, or don't you?" Fran said more anxiously than inquisitively.

"Well, they want to do another interview by phone with someone from their Human Resource department, although he said it was just a formality."

Later in the week, when Sean awoke Thursday morning, he was anxiously awaiting Mr. Trevors's phone call. When early afternoon arrived, and the call Sean was expecting came in as expected, shortly after 2:00 PM, he answered the phone, and the voice on the other end of the line asked to speak to Sean Freyers. Sean identified himself, and Mr. Trevors proceeded with the call. The questions Mr. Trevors asked seemed to be exactly what Mr. Dobson said they would be, nothing more than a formality. Mr. Trevors asked Sean if he was still interested in the positions and what his plans were with regards to how long he intended to stay with the company if he were hired. Sean answered the questions as honestly as he could, knowing that the future was not entirely in his hands, as he had always relied on a higher power to guide and direct his life. Sean's answers must have set well with Mr. Trevors because, at the end of the interview, he offered Sean a position with their company at an annual salary that would allow Sean and his family to live comfortably, even in southern California. Mr. Trevors explained that his company would send Sean a letter explaining the details of the offer, and Sean should read over and sign the letter, accepting the offer, and fax it back at the number provided. Sean thanked Mr. Trevors for the opportunity to speak with him and said he would be waiting for the letter.

When Sean hung up the phone, once again, Felecia was there with an anxious look on her face as she asked, "Well?"

Sean responded, "I think we're moving to southern California."

Felecia responded as Sean expected, using the same phrase she always did when life seemed to take a turn for the better, "I'm so happy for you," even though this time, for some reason, she had mixed emotions about leaving the cabin. Perhaps it was the uncertainty of what the future held for them next. Nevertheless, Felecia did her best to keep to herself what she was feeling inside, as she wasn't really sure what her true feelings were herself.

In the days that followed, Sean received the offer letter in the mail. He signed it, and the four of them began making plans for the move that was ahead. It was amazing how much the four had accumulated in the short amount of time they had lived at the cabin, and Sean felt it necessary to rent a truck for the move. Felecia didn't like moving again. The cabin was the closest resemblance to anything she could call home. However, she was keeping an open mind that maybe, just maybe, this might be the move that would give all four of them the opportunity for a new lease on life. As moving day fast approached, Sean was questioning in his mind whether the little fixer-upper of a vehicle that he had acquired with Nelson's help during his time at the cabin would make it all the way to southern California, especially since he intended to have Felecia drive the car while he drove the truck. Sean did what he could to best ensure that it would, and after packing the truck with everything they now actually owned, the four of them were about to begin the long trip toward what could potentially be a new life for them. Sean and Nelson said their goodbyes, while at the same time, exchanging information that would help them stay in communication.

Prior to the trip, Sean had somehow made sure that both vehicles were equipped with a GPS. Upon arriving in Seattle, they stopped and filled both vehicles with gasoline before heading south on the interstate that would eventually put them in the vicinity of their final destination, an apartment Sean rented sight-unseen after doing hours of research on Nelson's home computer. The twenty-hour drive took two and a half days, as Sean had never been one to keep driving just to get there. The timing of the trip somehow seemed to work out perfectly, as they found themselves arriving at the real estate office where they were to sign the lease for the apartment in mid-afternoon. After signing the lease and some additional paperwork, Sean and Felecia received the keys to what would probably be home for some time to come.

When the four of them arrived at their new home, they took the opportunity to see it vacant before moving their belongings inside. The apartment was a two bedroom, one bath, which meant that the boys would have to share a room; however, Felecia didn't expect Jonathan to stay there for long. Just over nine hundred square feet, this apartment was rather large for a two bedroom, one bath. The kitchen was a nice size and had a breakfast nook big enough for a dining table. The living area had a gas fireplace surrounded by stone. The master bedroom included his and her closets, and the boys room was large enough for two separate beds. Felecia thought to herself that she could be comfortable here. When the four of them had finished unloading the truck and the car, they decided on fast food for dinner because, at the moment, that was the easiest thing to do, as they were all very tired. They all retired early for the evening.

Sean had only one more day to spend with his family before starting his new job, so he did just that. In the weeks that followed, Sean found himself falling into what amounted to a daily routine with regards to work. Felecia began to become accustomed to her surroundings, and, although she would have preferred living in a house, she knew that was not something that would transpire in the near future. Jonathan actually found a job that allowed him to utilize the skills he had acquired in college. As time passed, eventually Jonathan was able to move into another apartment with two other roommates, and Sean and Felecia were left with just themselves and Jason.

Chapter 34

In the interim, the joint U.S./Canadian investigation had somewhat fizzled out; however, Agent Benson had no intention of backing off on the case. Although the courts were still battling over the release of the Alaskan Cruise Lines surveillance recordings, Agent Benson had already took it upon himself to continue with the Fruskin investigation without the Canadians, or the consent of his superiors at the U.S. Department of Justice for that matter. His determination to solve the Fruskin case led him to conduct an investigation on his own in every city that was a port of call for the ship the Fruskins had stowed away on, starting with Vancouver. As it turned out, Agent Benson only spent about two days in Vancouver, as his investigation seemed to be yielding no results. It seemed as though any bit of information Agent Benson received that could remotely be tied to his investigation resulted in nothing more than a wild goose chase. That same week, he left Vancouver and took the interstate south, heading towards Seattle. When Agent Benson arrived in Seattle, he wasted no time with regards to paying Nelson Fruskin a visit. Although the Department of Justice was not sanctioning his now rogue investigation, he had been able to gather information from his colleagues with regards to the department's first visit with Nelson, and that information somewhat prepared him as to what to expect when he arrived at Nelson's apartment.

Shannon was cooking when she heard a knock at the door. Although she didn't recognize the man at the door, Nelson was home, and she felt safe enough to open it.

When she did, she asked, "May I help you?"

Agent Benson replied with a question he already knew the answer to, "Shannon Fruskin?"

Shannon answered in a way that indicated she felt she was repeating herself, "Yes, may I help you?"

Agent Benson responded, "Shannon, I'm Agent Benson with the U.S. Department of Justice."

"Oh my God, we've been through this before. Look, as I told the men who visited the first time, what my brother-in-law and his family do with their lives is their own business. Let me get my husband."

As Shannon yelled over her shoulder for Nelson to come to the door, Agent Benson's curiosity piqued by Shannon's defensive attitude.

When Nelson arrived at the door, Shannon looked at her husband and said, "Nelson, this is Agent Benson, from the U.S. Department of Justice."

Knowing what was to come next, Nelson reached out to offer Agent Benson a handshake that anyone on the receiving end would believe was deeply rooted in sincerity. Years, of experience, however, had taught the agent this gesture.

As Nelson shook the agent's hand, he said, "Pleased to meet you, Mr. Benson. What can I do for you?"

Agent Benson continued the conversation, "Look, you both know why I'm here. Things will go a lot easier if you just answer my questions truthfully and to the best of your knowledge."

"We'll do our best."

Shannon looked at her husband with slight bewilderment as Agent Benson replied, "That's all I'm asking. Have either of you had any contact with your brother or his wife since our agents first contacted you?"

Thinking of his brother Kyle and his wife Kim who lived in Arizona, Nelson answered, "No, we have not," all the while wondering why he had not heard from them in such a long time.

"You do realize harboring known fugitives, especially those being sought in a federal investigation, carries a very stiff penalty."

"Yes, I do."

Although Agent Benson's gut feeling was that the two were not being completely honest with him, at this point he wanted to give both of them the impression that he was satisfied with their answers, in hopes that Nelson's and Shannon's reactions to their conversation might somehow spark a lead toward finding Steven and Fran Fruskin or their children.

Agent Benson ended the conversation, "If, by some means, you do hear from your brother or his wife, it would be in your best interest to contact me," and he handed Nelson a card and left, planning to spend a little time in Seattle.

In the days that followed, Agent Benson spent most of his time observing the day to day life of Nelson and Shannon, at least where they were traveling on a daily basis, anyway. At this point, both Nelson and Shannon had no reason to deviate from the day to day routines of their lives, and, as a result, Agent Benson's surveillance efforts were turning out to be fruitless. Something told him there was more to this, though, and he had no plans on ending this portion of his investigation just yet. He knew that at the moment, the U.S. Department of Justice was no longer sanctioning this investigation, as there were other matters that now took priority over this one, but he needed to gather the quantity of information he felt necessary to proceed. In a risky move, he contacted his colleagues within the department in an effort to gather the surveillance tools he felt he needed, and the authorization needed to use them. Not only was his request met with a high level of resistance, but Agent Benson was informed that his superiors no longer sanctioned this investigation. They also warned him that his resolve to continue with it may have serious consequences for him and the department.

Now believing that he was on his own, Agent Benson knew that if he wanted to continue what he started, he would be forced to take a slightly different direction. Realizing he was not making any progress through monitoring the day to day activities of Nelson and Shannon Fruskin, he felt it necessary to examine every possibility that might be a factor in giving him the slightest clue to Steven and Fran Fruskin's whereabouts. Something the agent just felt led him to believe Nelson Fruskin was not being truthful with him. Then, like a light bulb, it hit him. If he were in the same situation, a name change would certainly be in his best interest, and, for that matter, it would be in the best interest in the entire family. With that in mind, Agent Benson convinced a colleague he had worked with for years to search every database the department had access to that would yield name changes in all fifty states. That decision left Agent Benson scouring a slew of public and sealed records that would now require a great deal of his time.

After reviewing record after record, Agent Benson could not find any information that would indicate the Fruskins had changed their names. Now becoming rather frustrated, he was questioning whether continuing with this investigation was in his best interest. He had always maintained his determination for success in past investigations, and he somehow felt the need to continue. He would soon find out that his superiors at the U.S. Department of Justice did not agree with this sentiment. While purchasing what Agent Benson thought was a much needed cup of coffee in one of Seattle's many coffee houses, he was approached by two men in their mid-thirties, both wearing suit coats and ties.

One of them said, in what sounded like a question he already knew the answer to, "Agent Benson?" while also grabbing and pulling back Agent Bensons' right arm. The man continued the one-sided conversation, "U.S. Secret Service. Agent Benson, I'm placing you under arrest for ignoring a cease and desist order placed on a federal investigation."

Agent Benson was slightly familiar with the practice of members of one federal agency being instructed to take into custody a member of another, and thought it best at this point to just cooperate for now, not providing these agents with any other information. He was well aware that whatever his destination was, it would include an interrogation by whatever agency was deemed appropriate to handle such. He was placed in back of a white sport utility vehicle and driven to the Seattle airport, where they drove through a guarded gate and directly onto the tarmac. The vehicle stopped in front of a small private jet, and upon boarding, Agent Benson was placed in a seat near the rear of the plane. The jet was designed for comfort, yet, somehow, had an executive feel to it, as though it was commonly used to transport those of high stature.

As the jet taxied out toward the runway, Agent Benson had a feeling deep down inside that something wasn't quite right. It wasn't long before the jet was cleared for takeoff, the engines began their usual rev, and the jet began to speed down the runway, eventually lifting off the ground into the blue skies above. In very short order, Agent Benson was aware of the explanation for his discomfort, and it had nothing to do with the handcuffs he was still in. It didn't take long for him to realize they were flying over Canadian airspace.

Agent Benson looked at the two men in front of him who had arrested him confidently, and confidently said very emphatically, "U.S. Secret Service, my ass!!"

One of the men got out of his seat, walked over to Agent Benson, and, as he released the agent from his handcuffs, said, "We were well aware it wouldn't take long for you to realize you were flying over Canadian airspace. We apologize for the deception involved. However, both of our governments felt it necessary to accomplish our goal."

"Both of our governments?" Agent Benson asked in a tone demanding elaboration.

"With regards to the U.S./Canadian joint investigation involving the apprehension of the Fruskins, negotiations between our two countries have reached a conclusion that, for the moment, this case is not a priority."

"Would you care to elaborate?" asked Agent Benson in a tone like he was giving the Canadian agent a direct order.

"I can't do that, however, I believe my superiors can. For now, just relax, and enjoy the flight."

Agent Benson was quiet for the remainder of the flight,

perhaps in an effort to convey his displeasure with the way the situation was being handled. Four hours later, when the flight finally landed in Ottowa, once again they were met on the tarmac by a white unmarked sports utility vehicle and transported to the capitol building. Agent Benson was escorted to the office of Canada's Minister of Public Safety, and it wasn't long before Agent Benson had an opportunity to meet with Jason Culver.

When Mr. Culver walked into the room, he looked at the agent and said very calmly and in recognition of his presence, "Agent Benson."

Agent Benson responded, "Let's cut to the chase. Why am I here again?"

"Agent Benson, through higher-level negotiations, both of our countries agreed it is in both our best interests if we close the Fruskin case."

"Would you care to elaborate, Mr. Culver?"

"All I can tell you is that the situation at hand has been deemed by both our governments as acceptable."

"Mr. Culver, please understand my conviction that when I commit myself to an investigation, my resolve is to see it through until I have accomplished the goal set before me."

"Agent Benson, if you return to the U.S. intent on continuing this investigation, you will be arrested by the U.S. law enforcement agencies deemed appropriate to do so. While you are not being held by the Canadian Government and are free to return to the U.S., my advice to you would be to accept the hospitality of the Canadian Government and all our beautiful country has to offer for the time being. A vacation, if you will."

"I'll certainly take your words into consideration."

With that, the agent turned to walk out the door. He was escorted by the two Canadian agents. Jason Culver had no confidence that Agent Benson would heed his words, and he took the necessary steps to ensure that he and his office would be kept informed on the agent's whereabouts and actions.

Agent Benson had no intention of discontinuing his

investigation, but he now intended to pursue the case in somewhat of a different direction. He was now determined to find out exactly why both countries had decided to back off on an initiative they felt so important just a short time ago, and since Agent Benson now found himself in Canada's capitol, what better place to start than Canada's Department of Foreign Affairs. As he began to visit the Canadian agencies he felt might provide some clues to the answer he was now desperately seeking, it seemed that most of the people he contacted were aware of the Fruskin case, but had no more information than what he was already aware of. He basically received the same shuffle from agency to agency any civilian might find themselves in when seeking an answer to the questions they might have.

As Agent Benson continued to pursue the answers he felt he needed, he was well aware he was being watched. In an effort to temporarily stall the obviously steady stream of information on his whereabouts and actions being fed to Canada's office of the Minster of Public Safety, he decided to check into a hotel near the capitol building for the evening, intent on resuming his investigation in the morning. His ploy seemed to work for the time being, as Agent Benson was able to spend the night in a nice comfortable bed, while the Canadian agents in the SUV in the parking lot below had the privilege of drinking coffee all night in an effort to stay alert for the off chance that Agent Benson might leave his hotel room. When morning came, Agent Benson continued his pursuit for answers once again in Canada's capitol building. As he did, it seemed that when he put all the information he had acquired up to this point in order, it would point to what seemed to make sense. All roads were leading him back to Canada's office of the Minister of Public Safety, which only confirmed what Agent Benson suspected in the beginning. Jason Culver was not telling him everything.

Agent Benson returned to the office intent on speaking to Mr. Culver again. This time he had no intent of accepting the political rhetoric that Mr. Culver had to offer. He wanted answers. Although this time it took what could almost be called "an act of God" for the agent to be given the opportunity to speak with Mr. Culver again, he managed to accomplish it.

Upon meeting, Mr. Culver's first words were, "I understand you've been rather busy. What happened to you taking my words into consideration with regards to our previous conversation?"

Agent Benson responded, "Mr. Culver, there is a missing piece to this puzzle, and I am one hundred percent confident that you are in possession of it."

"And if I am?" Jason responded, cool and collected.

"My understanding is that this is a U.S./Canadian joint investigation, and as such, all law enforcement agencies in both countries are obliged to share the information deemed necessary to bring this investigation one step closer to its intended outcome."

"I'm afraid I couldn't agree with you more, Agent Benson. That is the very reason you were previously informed that as far as both the U.S. and Canadian Government is concerned, this investigation has come to a close."

"Look, the goal of this investigation..."

Jason cut him off with a rather stern voice, "The goal of this investigation was to protect the national security interest of both the United States and Canada. Nothing more. Both of our countries believe, at this point, that objective has been reached. Your personal desire to somehow fulfill some deep-seated need for more answers only serves to disrupt what now is an outcome that both of our countries can live with. Agent Benson, I'm going to attempt to be slightly more direct with you. How you choose to interpret what I'm about to say to you is a matter of personal discretion. Agent, I have a responsibility to my government and yours to protect the final outcome of this investigation. That being said, you can be certain that the sharing of information between our two countries with regards to this investigation will continue, just as you articulately stated previously. With that in mind, I am certain that the years of experience and the wealth of knowledge you have accumulated over the years would only lead you to believe that I have already done just that. So, on a personal note, if I may, it would be my advice to you to find a nice quiet spot here in Canada to quietly spend a few years. Should you choose to heed my advice, I can make the necessary arrangements to ensure that your lengthy stay in Canada is a pleasant one."

Ending the conversation with those words, Mr. Culver only had to look at his Canadian agents, indicating that they should escort Agent Benson out of his office and the building.

Chapter 35

As it turned out, Agent Benson's personal quest for more of a resolve to the questions he had was no match for Jason Culver's personal advice, and the agent returned to Seattle, where he intended to resume the investigation he had started. It didn't take long, and once again, Agent Benson was arrested for endangering the national security of the United States and neighboring countries, this time, by a legitimate U.S. federal agency. Meanwhile, after months and months, the litigation involving the release of the Alaskan Cruise Lines security tapes was finally coming to a close. The final outcome being a Supreme Court decision that when the release of data involved matters of national security, the right to passenger's privacy was not a valid issue. Alaskan Cruise Lines was subsequently ordered to release the tapes to the U.S. Department of Justice. By the time this occurred, the Fruskin case had already come to a close. The U.S. Department of Justice was well aware of the state of the Fruskin investigation, and subsequently, the tapes were only reviewed by those in a need-to-know situation. The tapes were then placed in a secure location.

As time passed, life returned to normal for the Fruskins, now going by the last name of Freyers. Sean was now well settled in his new job. Felecia had made the apartment home, and Jason was actually attending school. As the years went by, Sean and Felecia became rather comfortable, even to the point of redeveloping relationships with relatives.

What they didn't know was the United States and Canada knew exactly where they were at now, and they were both monitoring the Freyer's every move, including Jonathan's, using all the usual equipment that was available to them. This time, however, the United States and Canada's purpose was to keep the status quo. After all, what both countries wanted was for the events that occurred after the Fruskin's initial apprehension by authorities in Chartersville to resolve themselves. At least, that's what the United States wanted. Canada wanted to give the Fruskins an opportunity to live out a life as normal citizens, since it was Canada's conviction that all the so-called crimes the Fruskins were forced to commit were a direct result of the United States government actions. Although they may not have realized it at the time, the simple or not-so-simple act of changing their names in a manner that provided no public record, and choosing to attempt to begin a new life, resulted in the outcome both countries were looking to achieve. The time and expense it would take, however, to monitor this outcome in an attempt to keep things just as they are would prove to be an expensive proposition in the years to come. Eventually, both the United States and Canada gave up monitoring the Freyers lives, both countries believing that their goals had been accomplished and it was no longer needed.

Eventually, both countries would learn that "compleceny" is not a quality that would abode well for either of them. Back in Chartersville, a young detective determined to make a name for himself thought it would be in his best interest if he used his off time to try and solve cold cases. One that struck his interest was the escape of two detainees from a holding facility during a period when the city was supposed to be under a quarantine. It was noted in a report filed by the original investigating officer that a Chartersville patrol car reported stolen by an officer on the force at that time was discovered and abandoned in the same parking lot of the apartment complex where the escaped detainees resided. The report also stated that because the Chartersville police department was in a situation that required the full use of all their officers' services at the time, namely the quarantine, the stolen police car was not a priority at the time, since it could be returned to service immediately. The young detective thought this was a blatant miscarriage of justice, and he was determined to make it his personal goal to find those responsible. He reasoned to himself nobody should be able to steal a police car and get away with it. He was about to discover there was a whole lot more to this case than he expected.

The journey the young detective was about to embark on would lead him into a tangled web of information and misinformation that was much more involved than a simple case of a stolen patrol car. He thought he would start with a visit to the apartment where the Fruskins originally resided. Upon knocking on the door, he was greeted by a young lady in her mid-twenties, with long black hair, and slightly on the obese side.

The young lady said, "May I help you?"

The detective introduced himself as Detective Lannigan with the Chartersville police department and asked if she knew the former tenants.

She replied to the detective, "I'm afraid I don't. I've lived here for only about two months and don't know too many people. You might check at the office, though."

That, of course, was probably the first thing the detective should have done. When he arrived at the office, there was a young man sitting behind a desk who immediately asked if he could help him. The detective introduced himself and explained the purpose of his visit. The young man said he would be glad to oblige, but he wasn't sure if his records went back that far.

Upon looking up the computer files for the dates the detective had provided, the young man said, "Hmm. That's strange," as he stared at the computer screen.

The detective said, "What is it?"

"It says here that they were evicted for non-payment. However, the apartment was listed as abandoned with all possessions left behind."

"What would your complex have done with the contents of the apartment?"

"They would have been placed in a storage facility with

the charges being billed to the forwarding address."

"And if there is no forwarding address?"

"Then the complex will meet the minimum legal requirements for retention of belongings. In the case of this particular storage unit, that is the same amount of time this storage unit will allow for non-payment before auctioning off a unit's contents."

"Does your apartment complex pay the storage fees?"

"No, we do not."

"Why do you think I knew the answer to that question before I asked it? Just give me the name and address of the storage unit."

When the detective arrived at the storage unit, he asked to see the manager and was met by an older heavy-set gentleman with white hair. The detective explained the situation and provided the dates to the man. The man's response also indicated that he wasn't sure if he had records that far back. The man did manage to pull up the records and told the detective the contents were auctioned for non-payment.

The detective asked, "Who was the high bidder?"

The man responded, "Oh, I'm not sure I'm at liberty to disclose that information."

"I'm not sure I'm at liberty to allow the city to renew your business license. It looks like I see some zoning violations here."

"A-1 Holdings, 927 West Hodgins Southeast."

"Thank you."

When the detective arrived at the address, he was given, he discovered a large metal building surrounded by a very high chain link fence, a gate with a heavy chain, and a lock wrapped around. The lock was locked, but the chain wasn't fastened. The detective opened the gate and drove in. As he drove closer to the building, he could hear the sound of dogs barking. The dogs were secured in a pen behind the building, and there was an open door on one end of the building. As the detective walked in, the building appeared rather dark. There was a small area at the front with a high counter with a bulletin board and some clipboards behind it. There didn't seem to be anyone around, and the detective yelled out a hello in an effort to find someone. Appearing out of the large dark warehouse to the left of him was an older man, rather muscular with only a trace of short hair on his head, dressed in blue jeans and a muscle shirt.

As he approached the detective, he said, "May I help you?"

The detective expected the man to be less than cooperative, but he was pleasantly surprised when he told the man why he was there.

"We're a dispersing company. We sell what we can to second-hand stores. Some of what we can't sell is donated. The remainder is taken to the city dump."

After visiting A-1 Holdings, the detective realized that, at the moment, he was on a wild goose chase and thought it best that he pursue any lead that might pull him in a slightly different direction with regards to the case. Detective Lannigan's next move was to contact the officer who filed the report. Although the officer was no longer with the Chartersville Police Department, with a little research, the detective found himself taking a short drive east of the city into a remote area surrounded by evergreens and other trees. He traveled down a dirt road to reach his destination. The ruts in the road became deeper and more prevalent, and it became difficult to keep the department issued unmarked car from bottoming out in one of the ruts.

According to the information he had, the house he was looking for sat back from the road a ways; however, there would be a ranch style log entrance at the beginning of the driveway just off the road. As the detective pulled into the driveway, from out of nowhere, a dog began to chase his car. When he reached the house, an older man, not wearing a shirt, started to open the screen door. The detective yelled to the man to call his dog off. The man at the door yelled, "Chops!" and the dog retreated to the man and into the house. The detective got out of the car, walked up to the door, and introduced himself as Detective Lannigan with the Chartersville Police

Department.

"What can I do you for?" the man asked.

The detective explained he was looking for Jeff Peyton.

"That's my son. Is he in some sort of trouble?"

"I really need to talk to your son," replied the detective.

"Well, he's not here right now. Expect him back any minute though. He went to town to get a part for a plumbing repair. Gotta have hot water, ya know."

"Mind if I wait?"

"Do as you please. Mighty hot to be waitin' outside. 'Spose that's no concern o' mine though," indicating he had no intention of letting the detective wait for his son inside.

It wasn't long before the detective observed a white, late-model pick-up truck approaching the house from the driveway.

As the vehicle stopped, the man got out and said, "What can I do for you, detective?" immediately recognizing the department issued car.

"I'm here to ask you some questions about a case you filed a report on several years back."

"Which one might that be?" the former officer asked in an almost smug tone.

"It involved a couple of escaped detainees by the name of Steven and Fran Fruskin."

"I was just like you once. New to the force. After a year of riding with an experienced officer, figured I needed to prove myself. Make my name stand out in the department. A few years on the force taught me otherwise. You're playing with fire, detective."

That answer only piqued the detective's interest.

Recognizing the fact that the detective would have no intention of backing off on the case, the former officer paused for a moment and said, "Look, we all had our hands full. There was a report of a stolen car from a lot on Centers Boulevard. Some of us thought there might be a connection."

"Do you have a case number?" asked Detective Lannigan.

"Your a detective, aren't you?" With that, the man walked inside the house.

With just a little research involving stolen cars surrounding the time frame the Fruskins escaped from the holding facility, the detective easily narrowed his next stop down to a small, independent lot toward the east part of the city on Centers Boulevard. There were not very many cars on the lot.

As the detective pulled up to the small building in the center of the lot, an older man walked out the door and said, "So which one of these fine vehicles would you like to drive out of here today?"

"I suppose this one," the detective said, referring to the vehicle he was driving.

"Wouldn't be my first choice."

"I'm here to ask you about a car that was stolen from this lot several years back."

"And you're just following up now?"

The detective didn't see the humor and answered, "Look, can it. The stolen vehicle involved relates to another case, and I need your help."

"So, what do you need to know?"

The detective provided the man with the information he had with regards to the year, make, model, and the time it was reported stolen.

"Oh, yeah. I remember that one. I fired a kid over it. He was supposed to make sure all keys were secured before the lot closed. Customer left one in the ignition after a test drive."

"What else can you tell me?"

"They found the car in Vincent. No damage to it. Keys still in the ignition."

So the detective found himself headed toward the Vincent Police Department. When the detective arrived at the Vincent Police Department and showed his credentials, the officer in the records division was more than cooperative and provided the detective with a copy of the Vincent department's report. The detective drove to the exact location where the vehicle was recovered. When he got out of the car and looked around, he tried to imagine himself in the same situation as the Fruskins. Where would you go if you had just escaped from a holding facility in another city, and for that matter, had just stolen a car? It would have to be a place to hide or a place where you could blend in. The detective thought if it were him, he would want to keep moving. The college in the distance caught his eye, and he soon found himself at the dean's office, explaining the purpose of his visit.

"Oh, I remember that," replied the dean. "Young man by the name of Tony Barton. Had to expel him after a visit from the Department of Justice. Something about harboring a fugitive. Such a bright future, too."

"What else can you tell me?" asked the detective.

"Seems to me there was a young lady involved, too. I think her name was Kendra something."

"Do you have a last name other than 'something'?"

"Give me a minute," the dean said and walked into a room adjoining his office. He returned a short time later with a file jacket containing a manilla folder.

"What happened to modern computers?"

"These files are archived," the dean replied while flipping through the folder. "Hmm, let me see. Kendra Severs. The only relative she listed on her application was her mother at the same address as hers."

"What about Barton?"

"Oh, you're not going to find him. Shortly after he was arrested on the harboring a fugitive charge, the Department of Justice took him into protective custody."

"How do you know that?"

"Look, detective, Tony Barton was one of the best. He wanted the college's media department to see this thing through to the end. The U.S. Department of Justice had other ideas, and they made that vividly clear at the time."

Now well aware he was onto something much bigger than a stolen patrol car, Detective Lannigan headed to the last known address he had for Kendra Severs. When he arrived at the address, a woman that appeared to be in her late twenties, possibly even her early thirties, answered the door.

On a hunch, the detective asked, "Kendra, Kendra Severs?"

"Who's asking?" replied the woman.

"Detective Lannigan, with the Chartersville Police Department. I'd like to ask you about an incident that took place several years ago."

Much to the detective's surprise, the woman opened the door wide and said, "Come on in." She told the detective, "Sit down," pointing to the couch.

The detective said, "I'm fine," and remained standing.

As Kendra took a seat, she began to speak, "He ruined my life, you know."

"Who did?"

"Tony. Tony Barton," Kendra answered, elaborating and volunteering information without the detective asking for it. "After the story broke, I was expelled. No other school in the country would accept me. I had a promising future with the news media. Now I'm a secretary for an ad agency. I had a hard enough time just getting that job."

"What story?"

"You mean you don't know? Why are you here?" Kendra asked as if it made no sense for the detective to visit for any other reason. She continued, "Look, several years back, the college broke a story on the Department of National Security's trumped up bio-hazard scare they were using to prove to other agencies within the federal government that they could effectively quarantine an entire city without emoting civil unrest. When the story broke, it had exactly the effect the Department of National Security was trying to prevent."

"The Chartersville riots," the detective answered, now realizing exactly why the former officer he spoke with was so adamant about him not pursuing the case. "What happened to them?" he asked.

"The Fruskins? They just left. I had no idea where they went."

"Thank you for your time, Ms. Severs. If you have any additional information you can give me, please feel free to call me," the detective said as he handed her a card.

Realizing now that the Fruskins' only option would be to stay on the run, he reasoned to himself that they would need a car to do that. Since they now had a history of doing just that, lifting another one wouldn't be a problem for them. With that in mind, Detective Lanningan returned to the Vincent Police Department. His immediate task at hand was to learn if the Vincent Police Department had any cars reported stolen shortly after the story broke. Sure enough, they did. The one that piqued his interest was a 2007 Nissan Sentra that was recovered in a small, very small, town in Fort Brazen, Colorado. The report stated that the car had been recovered by the Sand City outpost of the Colorado Highway Patrol. Once again, no damage to the vehicle, keys left in the ignition.

The detective thought to himself that these folks certainly do not sound like professional car thieves by any means. That made him question the validity of the two being fugitives. When he looked up the status regarding the Fruskins, he found they were listed as fugitives, but the database made no mention of time served. He found that very unusual. When he arrived at the Sand City outpost of the Colorado State Patrol, his cellphone rang before he had a chance to get out of the car. The number on the screen was immediately recognizable.

When Detective Lannigan answered the phone, he immediately heard, "Detective, where to hell are you?"

The detective replied, "I'm in the process of investigating a cold case."

"Look, Detective, we have enough on our plate right now without having it spill over the edges with cases that have already been put on the back burner. Get your ass back here now."

"I'm afraid that might be rather difficult," the detective responded rather calmly.

The sergeant responded much differently, "Why the hell

is that?"

"I'm in Sand City, Colorado," the detective answered. He continued, "Look, Sarge, I need some time off."

"Look, detective, you're on thin ice as it is."

"Sarge, I promise, you do this for me, and you won't regret it."

Milling over in his mind why the young detective was promoted from street officer in the first place, the sergeant responded, "One week, Detective! Do you understand me? One week!!"

The phone went dead, and Detective Lannigan realized he was going to have to step up his game a little bit if he was going to comply with the sergeant's request.

When he walked into the outpost, there was a young trooper behind the counter. Detective Lannigan introduced himself.

The trooper replied, "You're a long way from home, aren't you?"

The detective explained he was there investigating a cold case from several years back and believed a stolen car recovered by their outpost might be involved in the case.

"Do you have a case number?"

Detective Lannigan provided the trooper with a copy of the police report he had obtained from the Vincent Police Department.

"Just a minute," said the trooper as he walked into a room behind him. He returned with a file in his hand, saying, "Had to dig for this one. Look's like that vehicle was impounded after it was recovered, by the U.S. Department of Justice of all things. There's an amendment to this report, filed by our department, that includes one Joshua Fruskin visiting this outpost in an attempt to locate his parents. It's dated shortly after the vehicle in the report was recovered. It wouldn't be of much significance at the time because the boy couldn't be held, as the APB was for his parents. The significant part of the report is that one of the officers involved at the time was suspended for divulging department information to civilians, namely, Joshua Fruskin."

"Would you mind telling me what that information was?" the detective asked.

The trooper responded, "Normally, I wouldn't, but it's a cold case, and you got a badge. Seems the trooper told him that the Wyoming Department of Criminal Investigation was investigating a case where they believed Steven and Fran Fruskin were allegedly spotted in central Wyoming."

"Thank you, officer," the detective said as he turned to leave the outpost.

"Good luck," the trooper replied.

The detective now found himself on his way to Cheyenne, Wyoming. When he arrived at the Wyoming Department of Criminal Investigation, the detective thought it best that he enter the building through the public entrance, as he was so far out of jurisdiction that it would obviously be presumptuous of him to entertain the idea that he should be allowed law enforcement access to the building. As the detective walked through the door, he found himself in a very small lobby area with the typical glass window designed to allow communication and provide protection for those on the other side. Detective Lannigan explained what he was there for.

The lady behind the window said, "Just a minute."

When she came back, there was immediately a buzz from the door to the right. The detective opened the door and walked down a short hallway to a second door, where he was let in and greeted by a man in his early forties, with short, already graying hair, wearing khakis, a long-sleeve shirt and a tie.

The man said, "Detective," as he opened the door. "I understand you're working on the Fruskin case. I thought that case had been shelved."

Detective Lannigan responded, "The case involves crimes that were committed under the jurisdiction of the Chartersville Police Department."

"As I understand, the case involves crimes that were committed under a whole lot of jurisdictions. What do you need to know, detective?"

"Just give me what you have."

"Last known possible location was a roadblock set up by the Montana State Police. However, a subsequent investigation by the same department revealed that the troopers at the road block may actually have let the Fruskins slip through their fingers when a search they were conducting of an RV was cut short on a call that the Fort Handlan Reservation Police had made a positive sighting of the Fruskins on the reservation. Turned out to be a wild goose chase. The three of them were believed to have crossed the Canadian border. Seems the U.S. Department of Justice just took over after that."

"Can you tell me who was leading the investigation for the Department of Justice?"

"Couldn't tell you that. However, this department was directed to forward any pertinent information regarding the case to an Agent Benson."

Knowing that he would make absolutely no progress with Canadian authorities, and believing that his only possibility with regards to continuing the case was obtaining information he could squeeze out of the Department of Justice, Detective Lannigan now set his priority on finding Agent Benson. When he contacted the U.S. Department of Justice, after speaking with about a half dozen different people within the department, he was told that Agent Benson was no longer with them. The detective's instinct told him something wasn't quite right here, and he was now more determined than ever to figure out exactly why that was the case.

The week his boss had given him was nearing its end, and the detective needed more time. He reluctantly called his sergeant in an effort to get just that. After a barrage, or what could be a hailstorm of not-so-pleasant speech, dotted by just enough of conversation to allow Detective Lannigan to decipher what his sergeant was telling him, he realized that he was granted one more week, and if he didn't comply with that deadline, he wouldn't have a job.

His sergeant ended the conversation, "Detective, one

more thing. What to hell is the Department of Justice calling me about you for, anyway! I just got a call from an Agent Benson. He said to tell you to stay out of Seattle. What to hell is that suppose to mean, anyway?"

Detective Lannigan now thought it was in his best interest to find the first flight from Cheyenne to Seattle. During the course of the two hour flight, Detective Lannigan took the opportunity to do some research on his laptop and discovered a Nelson Fruskin living in an apartment located in the northeast part of Seattle. After landing, the detective's first priority was to rent a car. When he arrived at the apartment complex, upon knocking on the door, Nelson's wife Shannon answered.

With the chain lock still attached, Shannon cracked the door open slightly and asked, "May I help you?"

Detective Lannigan identified himself. Only because Nelson was home at the time, Shannon opened the door and reluctantly let him in.

She yelled for Nelson, and as he came into the room, Shannon politely said to her husband, "Nelson, this is Detective Lannigan, with the Chartersville Police Department."

Although he knew exactly why he was there, Nelson still asked, "What can I do for you detective?"

The detective asked, "Nelson, have you had any contact with your brother recently?"

"Which one?"

"Mr. Fruskin, I'm going to make you a deal. If you don't take up too much of my time, I won't take up too much of yours. Now, can we try this again?"

With the recent visit from Agent Benson, Nelson felt his response to the detective's question needed to be a balancing act intended to protect his own family, while still giving his brother the opportunity to live out his life in a normal manner.

Nelson thought for a moment, and answered, "The last contact I had with him was a cabin about an hour and half west of here."

The detective noticed the pause before Nelson's answer

and suspected there was a whole lot more Nelson wasn't telling him, but his immediate objective was to follow the trail he had set out on. He believed what he might find at the cabin would give him more information than an interrogation of Steven Fruskin's brother at this point.

"Do you have the address?" the detective asked.

Nelson responded, "You would probably be a whole lot better off with directions, rather than an address."

"I'm fairly certain you can provide me with that information."

The detective now found himself on the same hour and half drive that had become so familiar to Nelson. After a jaunt down several dirt roads, the detective pulled off the road and onto a driveway that led to a heavily wooded and very secluded lot. Although the lot was overgrown with weeds, as the detective looked to his right, he could see what could only be described as an obviously recently renovated one-story cabin. The vegetation around the cabin was overgrown with weeds as well. As the detective stepped up onto the porch, he was already aware that the cabin was certainly vacant, and a peak through the windows confirmed this. The door was locked.

The detective was fully aware of the letter of the law when it came to the reasons that would justify him entering the building; however, he was determined to find some sort of clue that would allow him to continue with his investigation. The detective entered the building using the usual method that every street officer learned in the academy. He was rather surprised to learn that the cabin had two bedrooms in addition to the living room and kitchen area. A rather thorough search of the cabin yielded no clues as to where the Fruskins might have gone from there.

Recognizing the case he was working on at the moment was, at the very least, a sensitive one to the federal agencies involved, the detective had no intention of involving the Department of Justice again. Instead, he turned to the recent training that took place as to some of the methods used to further the investigation of a case. His first move was to obtain the phone records for the last known resident at the cabin. When the detective obtained copies of the phone bill, the fact that the name listed above the address was nothing more than the word "Resident" was all he needed to cement the fact that this was obviously the last known address of the Fruskins.

Although the phone bill was dated years back, the detective turned his attention to an attachment that listed incoming phone calls. The most current listed a couple of calls from a 310 area code. These calls seemed to stand out, due to the length of the calls, and the fact that these calls were isolated incidents. It didn't take long for the detective to figure these were calls from recruitment companies contracted by other companies to screen applicants by phone. When the detective made an effort to contact the recruitment companies by phone with his objective being to find out what companies they had contracts with, their responses were less than cooperative. Although time was running out for the detective, he believed he was just about to break this case, and there was absolutely no reason he should pause this investigation now, no matter what the consequences might be.

The detective booked the first flight he could from Seattle to Los Angeles, intent on visiting these recruitment companies personally. Detective Lannigan once again took the opportunity to do a little research over the course of the three-hour flight. The access he had to law enforcement databases enabled him to obtain physical addresses for the recruitment companies. After the plane landed in Los Angeles, the detective rented a car with on-board GPS and headed to the first recruitment company. When he arrived at the address listed for the company, he found himself in front of a ten-story building. He walked inside, and there was a courtyard with a water fall, plants, and trees, providing a peaceful outdoor look and sound to the surroundings. On the wall were flat screen monitors that listed the names and suite numbers of the companies in the building. The detective verified the name and suite number of the recruitment company and headed up to the eighth floor. When he opened the door to the company's office, he discovered he was in a small reception area with a counter directly in front of him, and some seats against the wall.

The receptionist greeted the detective with the standard, "Hi, may I help you."

The detective identified himself and asked to see the person in charge of records.

The receptionist responded, "Just one minute," and picked up the phone to call somebody.

A short time later, a man walked through the door to the left of the reception counter.

Upon approaching the detective, he said, "You must be Detective Lannigan. I'm Richard Freemont, Director of Operations. Is there something I can do for you?"

The detective responded, "I need to verify a call that was made to a number in the Settle area several years back."

"Let me see what you have."

The detective provided him with just enough information to allow him to comply with his request.

The next words out of the director's mouth were, "Well, our records go back ten years. However, we have a responsibility to our clients to keep them confidential. And, frankly, detective, I don't think you have jurisdiction here."

"Mr. Freemont, the case I'm currently investigating is of great concern to the U.S. Department of Justice. If you want to talk jurisdiction, I promise you, I can have the appropriate federal agencies here faster than you want to know. Things will go a whole lot easier for the both of us if I have your cooperation."

With that being said, Mr. Freemont seemed to be a bit more cooperative. With a little research, the detective was able to determine the call did originate from this office. Mr. Freemont stated that the client involved was a company by the name of Asher Technologies, but the call was placed to a potential candidate by the name of Sean Fryers, not Steven Fruskin.

"I need the address of the company," the detective told Mr. Freemont. Richard reluctantly provided the detective with the information, and it didn't take long for the detective to make good use of the information. Asher Technologies was located in the midst of several buildings in a complex designed to house office buildings. When the detective walked into the building, he once again found himself in a reception area and greeted by a young lady who asked if she could help him. The detective identified himself and asked to see Sean Freyers.

The receptionist responded, "Well, Sean works here. However, he's off today."

The detective responded, "Would you be kind enough to provide me with his address?"

"Oh, I don't know if I can do that," the receptionist responded apprehensively.

Detective Lannigan then said rather calmly, "Miss, Sean Freyers may have information related to a case I'm investigating for the Chartersville Police Department, and unless you have the time and money to spend defending a charge of 'Interfering with a Criminal Investigation', I believe it would be in your best interest to provide me with the information I'm requesting."

The receptionist did so, mostly out of fear, and the detective now found himself on his way to an apartment complex in what appeared to be a rather nice neighborhood. The detective found the correct building and rather cautiously knocked on the door. The door opened shortly after, with the chain lock still attached. Based on the pictures he had of the Fruskins from the original case, he immediately recognized Fran. She was slightly older, however, there was no mistaking the fact this was her. The detective then did more than just flash his badge and identify himself.

He purposely made sure Fran could see the words "Chartersville Police Department" on his badge as he said, "Fran Fruskin, I'm Detective Lannigan with the Chartersville Police Department. You know why I'm here."

Believing that the law had finally caught up with them, Felecia just unlocked the chain lock and let the detective in.

Still both standing, the detective asked, "Where is your

husband?"

At that moment, Sean walked in the room to see the detective standing there with his wife.

He asked, "Felecia, who is our guest?"

Fran just looked at Steven in a manner he had not seen before. Her eyes seemed to be filled with fear, while at the same time, looking to Steven for direction on what to do, as she said in a very direct voice, "Steven, he knows."

About the Editor

David Lewton was born in Albuquerque, New Mexico. He received his Associate's Degree in Computer Science from San Juan College in Farmington, New Mexico. Without David's skill and expertise, publication of *The Chartersville Story* would not have been possible.

About the Author

William Lewton was born in Medina County, Ohio and attended high school in the remote farming town of Loudonville, Ohio. As a sophomore in high school, William elected to include Creative Writing as part of his curriculum. The teacher would often allow students to share their work by instructing students to read an excerpt and pass their work on to the next student. William's watching other students work pile up on a desk while one of his classmates became enthralled with his work gave him a sense of pride. That teacher asked William to stay after class one day and suggested that he pursue writing as a career. During the course of the conversation she made it perfectly clear that she had told only two other students this in her entire career. She instructed William not to tell other students of their conversation. In 1977, when a writer's options were very limited, William took his teachers advice with a grain of salt. Over thirty years later, acting on his wife's encouragement, William used his free time, although somewhat limited, to write his first novel. *The Chartersville Story* took over a year to write. It is a suspense thriller that everyone can enjoy. The author sincerely hopes that you will enjoy this book and encourages your reviews.

Made in the USA
Charleston, SC
10 February 2012